the
FORBiDDEN
ROOM

Sarah Wray lives in Belfast with her husband and three
children. She holds a degree in Genetics from Queen's
University, Belfast, and has worked as a research scientist,
a childminder and a science teacher, as well as undertak-
ing voluntary work with disabled children. *The Forbidden
Room* is her first published novel. It beat thousands of
other entries to win the nationwide WOW Factor
competition, which was set up by Faber Children's Books
and Waterstone's to discover talented new children's
authors.

the FORBiDDeN ROOm

SARAH WRAY

First published in 2006
by Faber and Faber Limited
3 Queen Square London WCIN 3AU

Typeset by Faber and Faber Ltd
Printed in England by Mackays of Chatham plc,
Chatham, Kent

A CIP record for this book
is available from the British Library

ISBN 978-0-571-23072-3
ISBN 0-571-23072-5

4 6 8 10 9 7 5 3

For Paul, and Becca, Daniel and Christy.

the
FORBiDDeN
ROOm

Monday 6th June

I think they know that I'm on to them. I'm probably just being paranoid, but I'm sure that there's an atmosphere in the house. They're looking at me strangely, I know they are. And giving each other meaningful looks behind my back, I see them when I turn around. And they stop talking as soon as I walk into a room.

They know.

I'm sure of it.

And I'm really scared.

Who knows what they're capable of?

What they would do to protect themselves.

I've got to get away.

I've got to escape.

Tomorrow is the Queen's Silver Jubilee, there's going to be a street party. There'll be lots of confusion, lots of people. I'll go then. They'll not realise I've gone for ages. I could hitch-hike.

They'll never find me.

At least I pray to God they won't.

A few months earlier

Outside the one window high in the wall of the lab, the sky was dark. The particular blue-black darkness of the dead of night. Although the moon was full, its brightness was quelled by a succession of wispy clouds that chased each other to hide it. The effect was breathtaking. The clouds glowed golden and yellow, deepening to purple at their edges. Silver moon-rays escaped through chinks, making searchlights that illuminated ... nothing. Nothing but treetops, some night-time creatures prowling, looking for food, the dark quiet building that nestled behind the trees – and the window, the only other source of light, barely visible behind the bushes that grew around it.

Inside the lab, nobody noticed the sky.

Two figures moved with practised efficiency. They were measuring tiny amounts of fluids, mixing them, holding up the small test-tubes to the neon strip-lights to better observe the reactions taking place inside them.

Suddenly one of the figures slumped, dropping the tray she'd been holding. The sound of it spilling its contents shattered the silence of the lab, and as if the silence had been the only thing holding her together, she began to unravel. At first whimpering, and then loudly sobbing. The other figure, a man, hurried over to her. He placed his arm around her shoulder and she immediately stiffened.

'We haven't tried everything yet, but . . .' He gently turned her to face him and took her hand. '. . . we have to accept the fact that it just might not work.'

'NO!' she yelled at him as if he'd hit her, 'I WILL NOT ACCEPT THAT! IT HAS TO WORK.'

And then more quietly, in a voice that was almost pleading:

'It has to work.'

One

Jenny sat chewing the end of her pen, occasionally pausing to doodle on the corners of her otherwise blank page. 'Write about yourself.' That's what Sarah the care worker had told her. She'd been chosen as one of the children to be featured in the next issue of *Foster Carers*, the magazine given as part of an information pack to prospective foster parents. Like a kid catalogue. This season's special offers in troubled orphans or unwanted offspring.

How was she supposed to sell herself? 'House broken' or 'Has all her own teeth'?

The magazine photographer had already taken her picture: a head and shoulders shot. She had a copy on the desk beside her page. It wasn't too bad as pictures of her went. She didn't have horns or anything. She looked kind of normal. Not as cute as the little kids: at fourteen she was nearly too old to expect to be fostered. And then there was her disability to get over. Not that she minded too much. She'd got used to living at Oak Hall Children's Centre.

The centre used to be an old people's home, and

before that it had been a private residence. It was a beautiful old building, red brick with lots of chimneys, and although new wings had been added, they didn't detract from its settled look. The house was large, but balanced by the green leafy grounds and gravel paths around it that crunched comfortingly underfoot. The gardens held many secret paths and hidden summerhouses. Jenny had almost grown to love the place. Her mum would have loved it too; she'd always wished they could live in a big old house. Her mum's absence was the one bad thing about living there. Just one thing, but one big enough to make her feel sometimes as if she was wrapped in swirling black fog and that the ground was falling from under her. A pretty big bad thing.

'Jenny! Guess what? That new boy, Braden, has climbed the big tree and he's stuck and Sarah's going mental. She's about ready to call the fire brigade or something. Come and see.'

Hayley, Jenny's room-mate and sister-she-never-had was always excited about something. She could be a pain when Jenny wanted some peace, but she kept things interesting and she'd been the first to talk to Jenny when she arrived at the home and had been surrounded by awkward silences.

Jenny put down her pen with barely a flicker of guilt. She'd write the stupid thing later. She slowly followed Hayley out into the garden.

Jenny and Hayley's bedroom was on the second floor, but the house had lifts, a throwback from when it was an old people's home, Jenny guessed. Hayley had already run down the stairs by the time Jenny got to the top of them, but she must have pressed the button for the lift first, as it was lit up, and the lift arrived just as Jenny did. She got in, shouting as she did, 'Wait for me, Hay!'

The lift was wood panelled and quite small. Jenny fought with the feelings of claustrophobia that always tried to creep up on her when she was in there. Like she was trapped in a coffin. She was just starting to panic, when the lift pinged, and opened its doors on the ground floor.

'Come on, slowcoach, or they'll get him down and we'll miss it.' Hayley was bouncing from foot to foot, waiting impatiently for Jenny.

'Go on ahead, I'll catch you up.'

Indecision flickered in Hayley's eyes until she seemed to physically push it down.

'Don't be dumb,' she said. 'We stick together. Just hurry up, will you?'

Together they went outside, through the front entrance and down the stone ramp, and around the path to a grassy area to the left of the house. There was quite a crowd of children standing around a large oak tree.

Sarah was standing by the tree calling up to Braden, 'Hold on tight, there's help on the way.' She'd been a care worker for nearly ten years and could cope with most things, but still she looked flustered as she peered upwards through the leaves.

'Hey, Jen, hey, Hayley!' Jenny's insides leapt as she heard her name spoken by a familiar voice. Lee Chan was exactly one month older than Jenny and had arrived at the home on the same day as her, eighteen months ago now. He'd been out on short-term fostering stints, but had always come back. Jenny found herself pining for him when he was away – although she was careful not to make a big show of how happy she was each time he came back.

'Hey, Lee! What's going on with the new kid?'

She impressed herself with how steady her voice sounded when she spoke to him, like her body wasn't doing a tap dance from the inside out. Of course she could never tell him how she felt, would never tell him. She couldn't face his rejection, or pity – pity would be even worse.

'He got on the wrong side of Barry when he was in one of his moods, they had a bit of a slanging match, and then the new kid took off up the tree like he's a reincarnated squirrel.'

Barry was a large fifteen-year-old who had been at the home for a couple of months. Jenny hadn't really got to know him – he was quiet and closed – and she had once heard him actually snarling when someone got too close to him.

'It was impressive,' Lee went on. 'I didn't think it was possible to climb up a tree like this one.'

Jenny looked up past the thick trunk of the oak tree and through the leafy foliage. She could just make out the figure of a small boy clinging on to one of the horizontal branches. He didn't look so much like a squirrel, more like a frightened mouse, small and pale.

Sarah was still calling up to him. 'Braden, Barry said he's sorry he shouted at you. He was just feeling a bit cross, like we all do sometimes, but he didn't mean it.' The words that should be spoken softly sounded almost comical as Sarah shouted them up the tree loudly enough to be heard over the chattering of the other children. It was hard to tell if Braden was listening, as his face was mostly obscured by leaves. Everyone turned as a clattering came up behind them. It was Tony, one of the other care workers, carrying a stepladder.

Advice came from all sides about where he should place it, until, exasperated, Tony yelled at everyone to be quiet, then instantly had to apologise to Braden, who had scurried up to a higher branch.

As Jenny stared at Tony positioning the ladder, the scene blurred and changed in her mind to another tree, another time.

She'd been eight years old. Her mum, Eve, had brought her along to one of her tree-huggers' get-togethers. Jenny's mum insisted she called her by her first name even though Jenny would rather have just called her Mum. They were protesting against the building of a new by-pass through some woodland, and had set up camp on the edge of the copse of trees that was due to be cut down. Everyone seemed to be wearing rainbow-coloured baggy jumpers, and hair that was either very long or very short. It was like some crazy uniform that was a nod to every human's need to conform, even the non-conformists. Crystals were hung from trees, and a couple of guitarists began a jamming session. Someone had even had the foresight to set up a table selling hand-made jewellery to the curious onlookers. Jenny's mum had brought along some of her stuff to sell, stuff she worked on in the evenings, allowing Jenny to pick out stones and patterns, and claiming that she couldn't do it without her help.

For eight-year-old Jenny the experience in the woods was both exciting and alarming. If Eve had rebelled against her strict, puritanical parents by being wild and radical, Jenny's rebellion had been the opposite. She liked rules, she found comfort in order and structure, she wanted to conform. So doing anything even remotely illegal made her deeply uneasy. And to make things worse, her mother had taken her out of school to attend the protest. As she climbed a tree and obediently sat on a branch beside Eve, she had visions of truancy officers coming with stepladders to drag her down.

'Jenny!'

Jenny shook her head, to shake away the memory, and noticed that the other children were heading back towards the house. Sarah was looking at her with concern.

'You were miles away, Jenny. Is everything all right?'

'Hmm? Um, yeah. I was daydreaming, I guess.'

'I was just saying to the others that we should give Braden and Tony some space.'

Jenny looked at Tony sitting precariously on the top of the ladder, talking gently to Braden.

'Come on, I'll walk you back to the house. I want to

have a few words with everyone before Braden comes back in.'

As they made their way slowly back, Sarah asked Jenny how her piece for the magazine was going.

'Not great. What am I supposed to say?'

'I'll help you with it, after tea. Okay?'

'Yeah. Thanks.'

They'd arrived at the front door by then, and Jenny followed Sarah into the family room, where the others had been told to wait. The name of the room was supposed to remind the children that they were part of a family in the care home, a family where the 'parents' worked in shifts and brothers and sisters came and went. Strange family.

She went over to sit beside Hayley, and then looked up at Sarah.

'Well, thanks for coming, everyone,' Sarah began. 'I just thought I should tell you some things about Braden. Braden has a mild form of autism. Some of you will know what that is, but for those of you who don't, it just means that you have to give him space, and not be too noisy around him. He likes order and routine, and he doesn't like to be touched.'

As Sarah was talking, a scuffle had broken out between two boys over who got the cushion off the sofa. They ended up rolling on the floor hitting each other with it. Sarah rolled her eyes. 'Why central office thought it was a good idea to send him here, I don't know. But . . .' She raised her voice to be heard over the cushion fight, and stared at the offenders until they sheepishly sat back down, leaving the cushion on the floor.

'But, seeing as he is here, we will all do our best to make him feel happy and at home. Won't we?'

'Yes, Sarah,' the children chorused reluctantly.

Jenny wondered if a similar little talk had been given before she arrived at the home. Were the others told not to stare at her, to treat her as if she was normal?

'Wanna play Playstation?' Hayley asked her.

'No way!' shouted Ahmed and Dylan, two ten-year-old boys who shared the room beside Jenny and Hayley's. 'It's our turn! Sarah, isn't it our turn! We've been waiting ages. It's not fair, just because she's . . .' Ahmed's voice trailed off and he looked awkward.

'I don't feel like playing anyway,' Jenny said.

Hayley was never one to linger on defeat, and she quickly got enthused by a new idea. 'I know, let's make scoubidou bracelets. My gran sent me a big pack of threads. There's glittery ones and everything.'

'Yeah,' said Jenny, trying for Hayley's sake to sound enthusiastic, 'good idea.'

After tea, Jenny was back in her room, doodling on her page. The others were downstairs watching TV. Sarah had told her she'd be up in a minute.

Two years ago, if she'd been asked to write about herself it would have been a whole lot easier.

Name: Jenny Ackerman (actually her name was Jennifer Moonchild Firstjoy Ackerman, but she'd be mortified if anyone found out. She had begged her mother not to fill in her middle names on any of her school application forms, and had told none of her friends of their existence).

Athletic. She had been in the school cross-country running team, as well as the county youth team.

Part of a single-parent family. Her mum, Eve, had left home aged seventeen and set off to travel the world. She'd taken the ferry to France and hitch-hiked or worked at casual jobs to pay her bus or train fares around Europe. She'd told Jenny about the places she'd been to and the people she'd travelled with. The stories had sounded romantic: sleeping under the stars in Greece, picking grapes in France and oranges in Spain, hooking up with a guitarist in Italy and singing with him on the streets. Jenny wondered if the reality had really been as good as her mother made it sound. If 'sleeping under the stars' was just a euphemism for being homeless.

After Jenny was born, Eve had continued to travel for a while with Jenny's father, another Italian named Gilberto. But life on the road was a lot more complicated with a baby and Gilberto left her after a few months of fatherhood. She'd returned to England, but not to her parents – who Jenny had never met and now never would, since they died together when Jenny was ten years old, succumbing to fumes from their faulty gas central heating.

Eve told Jenny that bringing her up was an adventure better than travelling the world, and that she never regretted having her. But Jenny sometimes saw her sigh and look wistful when they watched TV programmes about places where she'd been before Jenny was born.

Jenny could have written about her hobbies. She loved to read, and was learning about jewellery making from Eve. Although Jenny was vegetarian at home with her mum, she secretly loved McDonald's burgers, and would sneak there with her friends after school. She wanted to learn to ski. The school was going on a skiing trip to France, and Eve had taken on an extra job, working in the twenty-four-hour garage shop, to save up for Jenny to go.

But that was then. She never got to go on the skiing trip, and now she never would.

Sarah knocked on the door and Jenny called for her to come in.

'Well,' she smiled, 'how's it going?'

Jenny showed her the page, which was now edged with doodles, but with a blank white space in the middle. She'd drawn a stick man skiing, and Sarah noticed the drawing and asked her if she'd ever been skiing.

'No,' Jenny said. 'I was going to go with school, before the accident. But then I didn't.'

Sarah looked thoughtful, but didn't say any more on the subject. 'Let's think about what you're going to write in the middle there,' she said. 'We could start with how you're very artistic.'

Jenny smiled, but her smile fell flat as she contemplated the page.

'Well, it seems to me', Sarah said, 'that there are lots of things you could write about yourself, but the one that you're worried will stop people from reading on is, well, your legs.'

Jenny looked down at the two stumps that were strapped into her wheelchair. They ended mid-thigh, one slightly longer than the other. She was wearing shorts, so the pink and brown mottled ends stuck out beyond them.

'So,' Sarah went on, 'you could start with who you are, what you like, then throw in your legs at the end, a sort of whammy, to wake people up. Or you could start with your legs, then if the prospective parents stop reading there, they don't deserve to know what a wonderful, interesting person you are from the legs up.'

'Or I could just throw in clues,' Jenny said. 'Like, I'm a wheelie nice person who likes to be pushed around, or, I always argue my point even if I don't have a leg to stand on.'

'Jenny!' Sarah laughed in spite of herself. 'How about: "Hi, my name is Jenny. I'm fourteen years old. Two years ago I was in a car accident and had to have both my legs amputated. I have a wheelchair to get around in, and also have artificial legs, although I don't wear them as often as I should."'

'Hey!' Jenny said. 'I do wear them. But they rub me and they're not comfortable, and it's hard.'

'Okay, I know,' Sarah said. 'Well, how about you change it to: "and I also have artificial legs that I'm getting better at using all the time". Happy?'

'Oh yeah,' said Jenny, 'I'm over the moon.'

'Ho, ho. Great sense of humour – there's another thing you could write.'

Jenny looked at what she'd written: '. . . both my legs amputated . . .'

She remembered when the doctor had told her, 'Jenny, I'm very sorry but we had to amputate both your legs.' She'd wanted to shout at him, tell him to stop lying to her. She could still feel her legs. She'd started kicking, or trying to, but she was tired and it hurt. So she sat up, just a little, and looked down the bed. Then she saw that the covers dropped away to nothing where her legs should have been. She wanted to drop away to nothing with them. To escape from the nightmare. 'No,' she'd said. That was all. No. As if it could change anything. As if that little word could make it go away.

She said it very quietly, and then she lay back down, her tears making tracks down the side of her face, tickling her ears.

'I'm sorry,' the doctor said.

'Jenny, hel–lo!'

Sarah was trying to get her attention. Again Jenny shook her head, looked back at her page.

'Now that's out of the way, you can write about the real you. Tell them about your reading, and your poetry. Tell them about your jewellery. I'm going to go back downstairs and fill in some paperwork. Give me a shout if you need any more help, okay?'

'Yeah. Okay.'

Jenny had started to write poetry when she was eleven. It had been about silly things at first, like boy bands and ponies, but she soon started writing things that were a little deeper, about her feelings and her confusions with life. It was a way for her to work things out in her mind, to find her own voice. After the accident she didn't write anything for a while, until the occupational therapist at the hospital suggested she did, and then, once she'd started, she could barely contain the thoughts and feelings that came from inside her. She filled notebook after notebook, scribbling poems that she wouldn't let anyone read. That she wouldn't even read over herself. Not yet.

There was a knock on the door and Jenny yelled, 'I'm doing it, Sarah.'

But it wasn't Sarah who peeked a head around the door. It was Lee.

'Lee,' said Jenny, quickly turning over her page and putting a book on top of it. 'Come in.'

Lee came in carrying two steaming mugs. 'Thought you might like a cup of tea.'

'Thanks,' Jenny smiled and took a mug.

Lee sat down on Hayley's bed and put his mug on her bedside table. He picked up one of her stuffed toys and started twisting its head around.

'She'll kill you if she sees you doing that.'

Lee looked at his hands as if he didn't realise what he was doing, and put the toy down self-consciously.

'Thought you were watching TV with the others.'

'I was – *The Simpsons* – but it's an episode I've seen lots of times. Besides, the little ones are fighting, and no one could hear the TV.'

'Did they set off the new boy again?'

'Braden? Nah, he's in the dining room on his own doing jigsaws.'

'You couldn't blame him for wanting peace from that lot.'

'Yeah, I know what you mean.'

The conversation petered out, and when Jenny took a sip of tea, the slurping noise made them both laugh. Lee opened his mouth and took a deep breath as if he was going to say something, then thought better of it and swallowed whatever it was. He did it again.

'You all right, Lee?' Jenny asked him. 'You look like a sick goldfish.'

'Yeah, I'm all right. I mean . . . no, I'm not. I mean, I dunno. It's just . . . Jenny . . .' He paused and his shoulders slumped. 'I'm getting fostered again.' He said it as if he was telling her he'd been given a death sentence.

'Oh.' Jenny forced herself to smile. 'That's great – isn't it?'

'It's the fifth time since I got here.'

'Well? That's five times more than me. You're very popular.'

Lee's eyes roamed the room, avoiding Jenny's. 'Very popular until they send me back. What's wrong with me, Jenny?' He looked at her now, and his eyes looked sad and questioning. Jenny didn't know what to say.

'Why do people keep sending me back?'

Jenny stared at Lee's smooth, tanned skin and dark Chinese eyes, and couldn't imagine why anyone would let him go.

'Who is it this time?' she asked him.

'I don't know. Sarah said she'd talk to me about it tomorrow.'

Hayley burst into the room just then, like a whirling dervish. 'Jenny, I just remembered I haven't done my English homework, and Mrs Kendal will kill me . . . Oh. Lee's here. With you. You and Lee together. I'll just go then.' She was backing towards the door, 'My schoolbag is downstairs. Yes. That's it. My schoolbag. Downstairs. Bye!'

The serious mood was broken and Lee and Jenny both laughed and rolled their eyes as Hayley left. Hayley knew how Jenny felt about Lee. Jenny hadn't told her, but she'd worked it out. She'd noticed how Jenny's eyes followed him about a room, how she moped when he left to be fostered. Jenny made her swear never to tell anyone. No one could know.

She wished she could tell everyone. If she was normal and Lee could like her, she would shout it out. She laughed with Lee at Hayley's behaviour, but there was nothing funny about the way she felt inside. She longed to be alone with Lee. She wanted him to kiss her. To stroke her hair and tell her he loved her. She wanted to take his hand and run with him through fields of flowers.

Hah.

She might as well want to grow wings and fly to the moon.

'You're a good friend, Jen.'

Good friend. Yeah.

'Sure, Lee. Any time.'

Two

Sarah was pacing up and down the hall trying to cajole a screaming baby, while two wide-eyed toddlers looked up at her. Their mum had had a car accident and needed to be in hospital for a week or two and the three children had been taken in for emergency care. One of the regular short-term foster carers would be turning up soon to collect them. Jenny was in the hall with them, waiting for the ambulance that came twice a week to take her to the hospital for physiotherapy. She was in her wheelchair, but had her legs tucked into the tray underneath the seat. She would have to practise using them with the physiotherapy team and she wasn't looking forward to it. Her artificial legs were clumpy and unruly.

She used to run effortlessly and gracefully. She'd been the second fastest runner in the county youth team, and her coach had said she had the best style. He'd said she ran like water flowing, smoothly, like she was born to run. And she *did* feel as if she was born to run, as if she was only herself with the wind in her hair and the track pounding away under her feet.

Now she was born to hobble.

She saw one of the toddlers looking at her legs. The child jumped down from her seat and walked over to Jenny.

'You can take your legs off!' the little girl said with awe. She looked at her own legs, as if expecting to see hinges or buckles on them. She stamped once or twice, and ran her little hands down to her ankles as if still not convinced. 'I can't take my legs off.' She sounded sad, as if she was the faulty one. 'Can I ride in your buggy?' She meant the wheelchair of course, and Jenny lifted her up on to her lap. The little girl screeched and giggled as Jenny did wheelies and spins with her chair. Then the little girl's brother wanted a turn. He was a little older and a bit more shy, but he was soon laughing as loudly as his sister when Jenny spun him too.

'Why do your legs come off?' he asked.

'Well,' said Jenny, 'I was in a car accident, and my legs got hurt, so the doctors made me new legs.'

'My mummy was in a car accident,' said the boy excitedly. 'Will she get new legs?'

'Oh, no, no,' Sarah cut in, having finally got the baby quiet. 'Your mummy just hurt her tummy, and the doctors are making her better.'

'Will she get a new tummy?'

Jenny and Sarah laughed, and then the carer arrived and Sarah was busy sorting out the handover of the children. She paused to walk with Jenny out to the ambulance when it arrived. 'You're very good with little ones,' she said. 'That's good because . . .'

Just then the foster carer called out to Sarah as she was strapping the three children into her car. Sarah quickly told Jenny she would talk to her later, and handed her over to the ambulance crew. As they pushed the wheelchair on to the hydraulic lift at the back of the ambulance, Jenny wondered what Sarah had been about to say, something about her being good with little ones. She hoped she wasn't going to be put on baby-sitting duties or anything like that.

The issue of *Foster Carers* magazine with Jenny's article and picture in it had been out for a couple of weeks now. Lee had left the day it came out. It turned out that the couple who had fostered him first just over a year ago had decided to take him back. Jenny had smiled and waved him off with the rest of the children in the care home. He'd promised to write and come and visit, but she hadn't heard from him yet. She guessed he must be happy. Without her.

It looked like Hayley was going out to a family too. Sheryl, another of the care workers, had told her a family was interested, and were being interviewed and checked out. Hayley of course couldn't stop talking about her new family. What their house was like, how they had a dog and a big car and how pretty the woman was. She prattled on and on, and Jenny smiled. She smiled but inside she crumbled. Always the same. The people she cared about left her. Left her behind. Helpless. Legless. Alone.

One of the regular ambulance crew, Jean, was making small talk with her. Jenny forced herself to pay enough attention to answer her, trying to keep her feelings superficial. She had been in bleak depression after her accident, and was scared to go back to that dark place in her mind. She had to move forward, not backward. But it was hard to see a future to move towards. What did life hold for her? Would she ever marry? Who would marry her? Would she ever have a career? Children of her own? How could she expect these things?

'. . . supposed to be a heatwave coming.'

'Really?' Jenny only heard the end of what Jean had just said, something about a heatwave. That was fine. Talking about the weather was safe. 'That's nice.'

'Right, young lady, you're all strapped in and ready to go. Hold on tight.'

The ambulance pulled away, its roof brushing against the leafy branches of the trees that lined the driveway to the house. They were hanging heavy with the previous night's rain, and drops of water fell from them in the ambulance's wake. Jenny watched them through the rear window and silently thanked them for shedding the tears that she forced herself to hold in.

Arriving at the hospital always gave Jenny a strange sense of déjà vu. The concrete ramp beside the stone entrance stairs. The mural of happy smiling families that lined the entrance hall. The plastic chairs arranged in rows in front of the reception desk. So familiar. So alien. Like she couldn't believe she had been here before, and yet so much of her life revolved around the place. The physiotherapy rooms were on the seventh floor. Jean walked with Jenny to the lifts and pressed the button that was too high for her to reach.

'You'd think they'd work out how to put the buttons at wheelchair height,' Jean said to her. Jenny smiled, waved goodbye and wheeled herself into the lift, which was already filling up with outpatients and visitors. A large man carrying flowers boomed at her, 'WHAT FLOOR, LOVE?' Like being in a wheelchair made her deaf.

'Seven.'

'RIGHT HO.'

People stared at her legs, and then pretended they were looking at something else. She was glad when most of them got out at the third floor where the canteen was. A mother with a child on crutches got in. Jenny recognised the boy from physio. He had lost a foot from a crushing injury. She wasn't sure what had fallen on him – she hadn't had a conversation with him, she'd just overheard snippets of what the doctors had said. The mother smiled at Jenny. The boy didn't. But Jenny understood. If you got too pally with the other stumpies, that made you more separate from normal people. Nobody wanted to join the freaks' club.

Physio was gruelling. Jenny's legs were checked to see if they were still a good fit. She had calluses from where the straps rubbed her. They didn't really hurt any more, but she used them as an excuse not to wear her legs.

She did exercises where she had to sit on the floor and flex her legs from the hip, sometimes on her own,

26

sometimes with the physiotherapist moving them for her, or holding them down so she had to push against the resistance. Then they worked on her balance. With two artificial legs attached above the knee, even standing still was difficult, and walking was a nightmare. They made her walk up and down between the parallel bars until she was sweating and crying.

The hospital counsellor had told her that losing a limb was like a bereavement, that you had to go through a period of mourning, and that for Jenny it was especially difficult because she'd lost both legs, and she'd lost her mum at the same time. All that grief. The therapist said she was not progressing with her prosthetic legs as well as would be expected in a girl of her age and fitness, and that the problem was psychological not physical. Jenny knew that that was true, but she didn't care. What was the point? She would never run again. She could get around in her wheelchair, so why bother with plastic legs? But the physios still made her try, still made her hobble about like an old woman, like the tin man in *The Wizard of Oz*, searching for the heart he wished he had.

'You need to wear your legs for at least two hours a day, Jenny. Okay?'

No answer.

'Jenny, I said . . .'

'Yes, okay. Two hours a day.'

The physio sighed and looked kindly at Jenny. 'I know it's hard, Jen, but with practice your mobility could be so much better. You could think about joining

27

a sports team, Paralympics . . .' Her voice trailed off as she saw that Jenny was frowning and looking away. 'Just think about it, okay?'

'Yeah. Okay.'

At night, lying in bed, Jenny listened to Hayley talking. Every night they chatted about stuff, whether Jenny felt like it or not. The need for quiet time was not something Hayley ever seemed to consider.

Sometimes they talked about school. They went to the same school, the local comprehensive, although Hayley was in the year below Jenny. Jenny missed a lot of school because of hospital appointments and had a private tutor to help her catch up. She used to be very conscientious with schoolwork before the accident, but she didn't care about that so much any more. She'd left behind her old school and her old life when she'd come to Oak Hall. She was glad in a way to leave her old school: going back so different would have been too much for her to bear, for the people who knew her as athletic and clever to see her deformed and deflated. At least at Northside High she was just 'that girl from the home in a wheelchair'.

The school had had ramps and automatic doors fitted the year before Jenny came, and she thought they were secretly pleased finally to have a use for them. They always included her in any publicity photos of the school anyway. Their token disabled person.

If she was the only disabled child in the school, at least she had Hayley to share the stigma of being a 'care-home kid'. Having to have permission slips signed by a guardian, rather than a parent. Having care workers come to the parent teacher evenings. Sharing that with Hayley made it easier.

Sometimes they talked about the other kids at the home. A lot of kids came and left after just a few weeks or months. Sometimes they went back to their families; sometimes they were fostered or adopted. Many of them had problems. And sometimes Jenny and Hayley would try and guess their stories.

For example, Hayley would say, 'I bet you that new lad's been knocked about. Have you seen how he jumps every time there's a loud noise?'

Or if a particularly thin and ragged-looking child came in, they pronounced 'neglect'. One new boy was secretly selling Gameboys and mp3 players to all the other kids, and Jenny and Hayley made up for him a family history of crime and corruption.

They talked about Lee sometimes, although Jenny wasn't comfortable discussing her feelings for him. They couldn't work out what his story was, why he was in care, and he'd never told them. He seemed too normal.

Hayley told Jenny her own story once, although in view of her reputation for imaginativeness, Jenny wondered how much of it was true.

Hayley, like Jenny, lived with just her mum. She had no memory of her dad, and her mum didn't like to talk about him. Hayley's mum was an alcoholic. Hayley remembered her being a lot of fun sometimes, laughing and joking and playing with her, but sometimes she was sleepy and grumpy, and sometimes she cried and Hayley didn't know what to do. She learned at a very early age how to look after herself, making herself drinks or sandwiches, getting herself dressed.

Her schoolteachers got worried, though, when she was often late or absent, or when she would come to school not wearing her uniform or with no lunch. Social workers were sent to the house, and called regularly to check up on them. Hayley's mum could usually maintain her composure with the social workers, but as her problem got worse she became abusive with them, or weepy, clinging to them and asking for help. Eventually Hayley was taken into care, and her mum was sent to rehab.

Hayley went back to her mum a few times, but always after a few weeks of staying sober, something would set her off and she'd have a drink – one thing would lead to another and Hayley would be taken back into care. Jenny was amazed that Hayley was so upbeat most of the time, as if nothing could get her down. But she guessed it was Hayley's way of coping, and she had once or twice seen what happened when Hayley stopped coping. Like the time Hayley decided to tidy up the family room. She worked really hard, moving furniture, dusting, sorting through piles of junk that had found their way into cupboards and on to shelves. Then Sarah, not realising what Hayley had done, got cross about an important letter she'd left in there that Hayley had moved. Hayley went ballistic. She screamed and shouted and threw things. She pulled the curtains down and knocked over the table lamps; she swept books off shelves and even pushed over the TV set. Sarah left her to it for a while, then went in and talked to her. Jenny didn't know what she said, but after about half an hour, Sarah and Hayley started tidying up the wreckage of the room together, and the other kids, who had kept a safe distance, heard them laughing and joking with each other as they did it.

Recently all Hayley could talk about was how things were going to be in her new home. That night she told Jenny she would talk her new parents into fostering Jenny too, and they could be real sisters. Jenny stared at the ceiling above her bed and wondered if she could allow herself to hope that that would ever happen. Of course not. Why would they want her? She didn't deserve a happy family anyway, not after what she'd done to her mum. She snapped at Hayley to stop being so stupid and stop going on about it. 'Well, excu-u-use me!' Hayley said, lapsing into a silence that lasted all of two and a half minutes, before starting again. 'I bet they would though, Jen. They're really rich, they could afford a special car and all that, and they're dead nice. I bet if I asked them, they would.'

Jenny sighed. She felt guilty for snapping, so she tried to be nicer to Hayley. 'Thanks, Hay. Sorry about before, I've just had a bad day.'

'S'all right,' said Hayley, easily mollified. As she chatted on, Jenny let her words wash over her, and tried to relax her body.

Lying in bed was when Jenny felt her legs most. Itching or aching, or just being there. She dreamt about them. Sometimes she would dream that she was running a race, and half-way through it her legs just fell off, and she was left lying in the track with the other runners running over her. Sometimes she saw severed legs walking around on their own, and that really freaked her out. Sometimes she was crawling on her hands and stumps across a room that seemed to go on and on for ever. A lot of times her dreams were normal. She had legs like normal people, and her mum was alive. She would be in her old house or her old school, doing normal stuff. And when she woke up, in the fuzzy time between dream and reality, she'd think it was true, and then she'd have to go through the shock and bereavement all over again as wakefulness brought her memory back. She was glad of Hayley prattling on at bedtime, helping her fight her fear of sleep.

That night she dreamed of snow. She was building a snowman with her mum. A huge snowman. She had to climb on her mum's back to reach the top of it. And as she stood on her mum's shoulders, her mum sank into the snow. Lower and lower until Jenny was just standing on the ground and her mum was gone. And Jenny was alone with the huge snowman. And the snowman just stood there not helping. She yelled at it, 'YOU'RE NOT HELPING!!!' And the yelling must have woken her up because then she was in bed, sweating and shaking and needing the toilet. She swung her legs out of bed, and remembered just too late that they weren't there. Hayley mumbled something in her sleep, but didn't wake as Jenny thumped to the ground. She whimpered, more out of self-pity than pain, then resignedly dragged herself across the floor to the en suite bathroom that was only yards from her bed.

The bathroom had sloping bars beside the toilet and Jenny used her strong arms to haul herself up. She could balance on her stumps beside the sink to wash, and as she peered over the edge of the sink into the mirror she thought she looked like a little child again, seeing the world from half-way up.

She crawled back to bed. It was three o'clock. Hayley was snoring gently. Jenny wondered if she would get a new room-mate when Hayley left, or whether she would have to face the horrors of the night alone.

If she dreamt any more that night, she'd forgotten it by morning, with the mad rush of getting ready for school. The school bus came to pick her up – another of the school's disability-friendly facilities that got to be showcased with her. She got notes from a girl in her class for the things she'd missed the day before. Biology: something about DNA fingerprinting – there were page numbers from the textbook for her to read and a worksheet for her to fill in. English lit: she'd already read the novel, so that was okay. Home economics: well, she was glad she'd missed that. The HE kitchens were not well designed for her wheelchair. Theoretically she was supposed to wear her legs for HE, but more often than not she 'accidentally' left her legs at home those days, as well as the ingredients for whatever it was she was supposed to be cooking. The HE teacher let it slide; she would let Jenny get on with her homework, but the care workers at the home would give her a hard time about it. 'It would help you when you get a place of your own, practising cooking *and* wearing your legs. You should at least make an effort.'

Yeah, yeah. Whatever.

Today she had maths (that was fine – maths was okay, if not terribly thrilling), and art (which was good – Jenny loved art, especially making models or sculptures). After lunch was PE. PE used to be fine, another chance for Jenny to get ahead with her homework. But the school had thought it would be great to send all the PE teachers on a course in integrating disabled students into school sports, and now she had to go to the gym and do 'activities specially designed for her needs'. Some of it was okay, though: the school had bought a 'polybat' table, which is like a converted table-tennis table, with raised sides and a rectangular bat with which Jenny could play from her wheelchair. She actually quite enjoyed those games, and the other kids liked playing it with her too, especially if it got them out of a cross-country run or something like that.

Coming home on the bus Jenny felt quite happy for once. She'd had an okay day. Hayley was full of gossip about who had fallen out with whom in her class, and Jenny indulgently listened. When the bus pulled up the driveway to Oak Hall, Sarah was standing waiting for it. She helped the bus driver get Jenny's wheelchair down, then said, 'After you've done your homework, Jen, strap your legs on and we'll go for a walk round the garden, okay? I want to talk to you about something.'

Three

It was warm in the garden. June was nearly over, and although the summer had started coolly, Jenny could see signs of the predicted heatwave. She leaned on Sarah's arm as she took awkward steps, using one crutch with her other arm to steady herself. The crutch made an extra footstep sound in the gravel of the path: crunch, crunch, crunch. Crunch, crunch, crunch. Like Jake the peg with his extra leg.

They walked in silence for a while, and then Sarah asked her, 'Jenny, how would you feel about going out to a foster home?'

'A foster home?'

They stopped at a stone bench that was almost hidden within the canopy of a weeping willow tree. Under the branches it was cooler and the light was strangely green. Jenny sat gratefully, her articulated knees bending primly.

'There's a family –' Sarah went on. 'They live not too far away. They have a son called Stephen, who's five . . .' Sarah paused for a moment and Jenny remembered something she had said to her that morning, about her being good with little ones. Sarah went on, cutting through her thoughts, 'They had two other children who were disabled, so their house is wheel-chair friendly . . .'

'Had?' Such a tiny word and yet with such a huge meaning. She had had a mum, she'd had a dad too, a dad who she didn't even remember. Now she had nothing.

'Hmm?'

'You said they *had* two other children. What happened to them?'

'Their two older children, two girls, had an illness that attacks the nervous system. They . . . well . . .'

'They died?'

'Yes.'

'Oh no,' said Jenny. 'That's terrible.'

'It is, Jenny,' Sarah said, 'but they seem to have come to terms with their loss now, and they want to foster. They've had a couple of short-term care stints, and the children they've fostered have been very happy there. In fact Lee was with them for a while before Christmas.'

Jenny tried to remember the different things Lee had told her about homes where he'd been. She didn't remember anything bad about any of the foster homes, except that they always sent him back.

'Well,' Sarah went on, cutting through her thoughts again, 'they read your article in the magazine, and feel that they'd like to foster you. Mrs Holland said you sounded lovely, and she really hopes that you'll want to stay with them. So, what do you think?'

What did she think? Jenny was so settled into the

idea that no one would ever foster her that she'd never really considered it. Did she want to leave Oak Hall? Leave Sarah? She knew Sarah was just one of the staff, that she might move jobs, or leave to have a family of her own, but she was the closest thing Jenny had to a mum now. The others were leaving, though: Lee had already gone and Hayley would be going soon. She could be part of a family. With a little brother. And they had lost children, so they would understand about grief, about how it never went away.

'I dunno,' she said.

'Well, think about it, okay?' said Sarah, smiling. 'Oh, there's another thing I wanted to talk to you about. It's very exciting.'

'More excitement?' said Jenny. 'I don't know if I could take it. It's as well I'm sitting down, 'cos my legs might just fall off with all this excitement.'

Sarah rolled her eyes. 'No, listen. It was interesting what you said to me about skiing . . .'

'Did I say something about skiing?'

'Yes, remember a couple of weeks back, when you were writing your piece for the magazine. It reminded me of a conversation I'd had with Dr Evans, at the hospital.'

'Dr Evans?' Dr Evans was a specialist in limb loss. He worked with amputees, and had done groundbreaking studies on all aspects of their care from pre-surgery through to aftercare and follow-up. It had been Dr Evans who first broke the news to her about her legs. 'Is he going skiing?'

'No – well, maybe – but listen! Dr Evans was telling me about his trip to America. You know he was away for a couple of months? Well, he was staying at a hospital in Seattle that has the country's leading prosthetic limb unit, and he was telling me about a programme there where teenaged amputees are taken skiing every year. They have designed special skis that you can use with your artificial legs, and Dr Evans was talking about applying for funding for a similar programme here. He's quite hopeful that he might get a grant from the Lottery fund, and if he does, he said you would be an ideal candidate for being in the first group of skiers. What do you think of that?'

Skiing. It had been skiing that had got her into this mess, in a way. She'd been so desperate to go on the school skiing trip, even though Eve told her they couldn't afford it. She'd begged and pleaded, and Eve had relented, taking the extra job in the evenings to earn enough money to pay for it. She'd agreed that it would be a great experience for Jenny, maybe bring her out of herself a bit. Then the school had sent home a note listing all the things she'd need to bring with her. Eve had read the note and sighed sadly. 'I'll have to work extra shifts,' she'd said.

Jenny hadn't thought about what all the extra work was doing to her mother. Looking back, she can remember how tired Eve looked, red-eyed and drawn, but at the time she was just excited about buying ski clothes, about who else was going on the trip and what they were bringing. She didn't stop to think.

She'd read about the accident in a newspaper that had been accidentally left in her hospital room by one of the cleaning staff:

> Single mother Eve Ackerman (30) was exhausted from doing two jobs, and it seems likely she fell asleep at the wheel. The car drifted out of its lane and into oncoming traffic. Ms Ackerman was killed instantly and her twelve-year-old daughter, who was in the passenger seat, suffered severe injuries and is now in a stable condition in hospital. Miraculously, although the car that Ms Ackerman drove into, a green Ford Mondeo, suffered extensive damage, the driver was uninjured except for suffering from shock . . .

'Jenny, what do you think?'

'Hmm?'

What *did* she think? On the one hand, Jenny really wanted to learn to ski, especially now that normal walking was so slow and plodding for her. But on the other hand, she felt that she didn't deserve it. By being selfish, she'd killed her mother. Why should she get what she wanted now? But Eve had wanted her to go skiing, hadn't she? She'd worked for Jenny to have that opportunity. If Jenny passed up on it now, would that make Eve's death even more of a waste?

'Jenny?'

'I . . . um, I . . . yeah, I'd like to.'

'Good. That's great, Jenny. But you can guess what I'm going to say now.'

Jenny guessed it would be something to do with her legs.

'You've got to learn to walk before you can fly, Jenny – it's really important that you practise with your legs. You need to be confident and comfortable with them or Dr Evans said he couldn't take you. Okay?'

Jenny suddenly felt something lift inside her. It was as if this was a way to get what she wanted without the guilt. Because she had to work for it. She would wear the blasted legs and hope they hurt. She would be humiliated and tired and sore, and if she managed to get through it, then she would ski.

'Yeah,' she said, 'yeah, okay.'

She was hobbling around the garden one week later, when a voice made her gasp and almost fall.

'Jen.'

'Lee! What are you doing here?' The huge grin that had taken over her face fell and she said, 'They didn't send you back, did they?'

'Not this time, hopalong. I'm just here for a visit.'

She stared at him, not knowing what to say, too pleased to see him to be bristled by his 'hopalong' comment.

'Where's your wheels?' he said. 'I thought I was going to be able to come and push you around.'

Jenny put a smile on her face, and used all her will to walk smoothly over to Lee. She dropped her crutches and put her hands on his shoulders and pushed, making him stumble backwards. 'Now who's pushing who around?'

Lee laughed, and said, 'I'll race you then.'

'Lee!'

Jenny tried to run, but lost her balance and fell. Lee turned around and came back for her. He held her hand and helped her back up. 'Truce?' he said.

'Yeah,' Jenny smiled and tried not to stare at the hand that Lee was still holding. He passed her one of her crutches, and kept hold of her other hand. They walked together further down the garden and away from the house.

Suddenly Lee stopped walking, making Jenny almost fall again. He steadied her and looked into her eyes. 'I miss you,' he said.

Did he? Did he really miss her? Did he miss her in the way she missed him?

'Me too,' she said. 'I mean, I miss you too.'

They stood like that, and Jenny wished she knew what he was thinking, wished she knew what he really felt for her, so she could tell him that she loved him, that she yearned for him. But instead they broke eye contact, looked away, embarrassed, and continued walking.

Jenny had been tired before Lee arrived – she'd already been on her legs for more than an hour – but she didn't want this walk to end. They talked about the other children in the home. Lee told her about the family that had fostered him. He seemed happy, and the time passed quickly. All too soon, Sarah came and found them and told Lee his foster parents were ready to leave now. It was only after he left that Jenny remembered she wanted to ask him about the family that were fostering her.

★

She would find out soon enough, as it turned out. Because Mr and Mrs Holland had already fostered, their application went through quickly and Jenny ended up leaving Oak Hall before Hayley did.

She went on an outing with the family a week before the day she was due to move in with them. She'd met them before, but only briefly once or twice in Sarah's office, so as she waited outside the front door of Oak Hall, she was nervous about what they would think of her and about what she would think of them.

Mrs Holland hugged her when they came to pick her up. She smelt nice: she wore a fresh floral perfume, and underneath it she smelt clean, almost clinically clean. Her hair was shoulder-length and dark blonde. Jenny tried not to compare it with Eve's hair, which had been a similar colour but short and spiky. Did she want this woman to replace Eve for her? Or even Sarah? She wasn't sure what she wanted.

Mr Holland didn't hug her. He smiled shyly and offered her his hand to shake, but then, thinking better of it, he withdrew it and put it into his pocket. He had short dark hair and a neat moustache and looked as if he was in his early forties. Jenny wondered if he looked anything like her real dad, Gilberto.

Eve had not even had a photograph of Gilberto to show Jenny, although she'd told her stories about him. The stories were always filled with laughter about the crazy things they'd done together. Eve had obviously forgiven Gilberto for leaving them, but Jenny didn't feel able to. She was angry more for her mother's sake than for her own. This man that Eve had loved had let her down, put his own selfish desires before hers. Jenny wanted no part of him. At least on the surface that's how she felt, but deeper down she wished she could remember him, could at least picture his face. And part of her was horribly afraid that the selfish side of her father, the side that made him leave her and Eve, was in her too. After all, didn't she put her own selfish desires before her mother's? Didn't she let Eve down? Was she cursed with the character flaws of a man she never knew?

'We hope you'll be very happy with us, Jenny,' Mr Holland was saying. Jenny smiled, telling herself not to blame him for what Gilberto had done.

'Thank you,' she said.

The little boy, Stephen, had been left in the Hollands' car and he was waving frantically at her through the window. He looked eager and full of life, like a puppy, and Jenny couldn't help returning his grin as she got into the car beside him. He was shy for a little while with her, turning his head away and sneaking bashful glances, but she made him giggle by pulling faces at him when he looked and soon he forgot his nerves and started chatting away to her.

They went for a picnic in the park. She helped Stephen to feed the ducks, and sat on a bench with Mrs Holland and watched Mr Holland pushing Stephen on the swings. 'Call us John and Helen,' they'd told her, like she was destined to be on first-name terms with all the parent figures in her life. John and Helen. John worked in some sort of medical lab. Helen had worked there too – that's where they met – but she had given up work when she had the children. Now she made ceramics and sold them on the internet. She told Jenny that it had started as a hobby, but lots of people wanted to buy her work and now it was a proper business. Jenny liked this about her: it reminded her of Eve, making jewellery to sell. She hoped she would be allowed to make some pieces too.

When they left her back at the home, Jenny started packing straight away. Her sadness at leaving Hayley and Sarah and her nerves at moving in with the Hollands were almost overtaken by excitement as she waited for her last week at Oak Hall to pass.

The week passed quickly and before she knew it she was hugging Hayley goodbye. The Hollands collected her from the home in a people carrier adapted for her wheelchair, although she was using it less and less now that she finally felt motivated to use her prosthetic legs. She had just one large suitcase with all her things in it, as well as a carved wooden box that had been Eve's. When Eve died, Jenny had asked if most of their stuff could be kept in storage until she was older. She'd picked out a few things, including the box that contained Eve's jewellery-making equipment, but the rest had been loaded into tea chests and locked in a storage shed to gather dust. Perhaps she should have just given it all away to charity, or burned it, or something. But somehow she didn't want to. She wanted to keep something of their old life. Preserved. As it was.

The drive to the Hollands' house didn't take too long, although it took them to streets that Jenny was not familiar with. They drove out of town and down a winding country lane. The car slowed and signalled left although Jenny couldn't see any turning, only thick woods to the side of the road. It wasn't until the very last minute that she saw the lane, little more than a dirt track that turned sharply off the road and through the trees. There was a large convex mirror attached to a tree at the corner, so that anyone driving out could see oncoming traffic, but no signs indicating a street name, or the fact that there was a house at the end of the lane. John drove slowly, to minimise bumping, although the surface wasn't too bad. Jenny spotted at least three squirrels scurrying up and down trees. and one actually leapt from a branch overhanging the lane to another branch on the other side.

'Look!' said John suddenly, slowing the car even further so that it was hardly moving at all. He pointed through the trees to the right of the lane. Jenny looked, and just saw the flash of white at the tail end of a roe deer as it trotted off through the woods.

We must be in the middle of nowhere, Jenny thought. She'd seen squirrels before, but never a wild deer.

John picked up speed again, and when the lane bent around to the right, Jenny saw a large opening in the trees and a big old red-brick house.

The house was half covered with ivy, making it look like it had grown there, like it was part of the forest. It had a grey slate roof and pretty dormer windows and was topped with several chimneystacks. Stone steps led up to a large front door that was flanked on both sides by bay windows. On one side of the bay windows were the doors to a built-in double garage, and on the other side there were more windows on what might have been an extension, added to the house at some point in the past.

John drove past the garage and around to the back of the house, where he parked the car under a canopy.

The house was much brighter at the back. Whoever had built it had reclaimed a large area of land to make a garden, a sunny oasis in the dark forest. The land sloped upwards slightly, away from the house, and a stream ran down one side, separating the lawn from mature flowerbeds that looked vibrant in the light reflected off the water's sparkling surface.

Jenny loved the house and the garden, and smiled as Helen helped her out of the car. She was wearing her legs, but a manoeuvre like getting out of a car seat was complicated, and she couldn't use her crutches in the confined space. John was un-strapping Stephen, who was bursting to get out. 'If you don't keep still, Stephen, I won't be able to unfasten your seat belt!' John said, trying to calm the squirming child. Stephen took in a deep breath and held his little body perfectly still until the seat belt was clear of him and his booster seat, then he climbed through the car to Jenny's side, and burst out of her door so fast that he almost knocked her over.

'Can I show Jenny around, can I, Mummy, can I?

Can I show her my swing and my sandpit and my bed-room and the TV and my new red car and . . .'

'Whoa, slow down, Stephen,' Helen said, laughing. 'Maybe Jenny would like to see her room first, or maybe she'd like a rest.' She looked at Jenny question-ingly.

Jenny smiled and shook her head slightly. She turned to Stephen and said, 'Would you show me your room and then my room please? I'd like that.'

'Yes, yes, yes!' said Stephen, bouncing up and down. 'And Mummy said we're having pasta and ice-cream for dinner. Do you like ice-cream, Jenny? I like ice-cream and chocolate and sausages and smiley faces and . . .' Stephen prattled on. Jenny smiled; she couldn't help comparing him with Hayley. She'd thought she would miss Hayley's endless chatter, but she started to think that that wasn't going to be possible: she would be too distracted by Stephen.

They entered the house through the back door, into the kitchen that was light and airy with windows over-looking the garden. The kitchen opened into a family room with dining table and chairs and a sofa and book-cases. John sat down on the sofa, and Helen pottered about in the kitchen as Stephen led Jenny through the family room and along a wide corridor to his bedroom. She couldn't quite keep up with him and he was already talking by the time she made it to his room.

'. . . and this is the aeroplane that me and Daddy made, and this is my teddy from when I was little, and this is my big-boy watch, and this is my bed with the blue cover that I like best, 'cos the other cover is in the wash from when I spilled my juice, and . . .'

'Who's that?' Jenny asked, pointing at a picture on the wall beside Stephen's bed.

'That's me when I was a little tiny baby!' Stephen said, as if it was silly of her not to know that. 'And that's my sisters who died.' Stephen didn't sound sad when he said that, just matter of fact. Jenny looked at the two girls. They looked about three and five. Pretty girls with curly hair and smiling faces. The older one was in a wheelchair. She must already have been sick, Jenny thought, when the photo was taken. She wondered how long ago the girls had died. It couldn't have been that long ago if they were both alive when Stephen was a baby.

'Would you show me my room now?' Jenny asked Stephen. He looked disappointed to end the tour of his room, but agreed, and led her along the hall to another door. Stephen and Jenny's bedrooms were on the ground floor, although the house had a small lift that had been fitted when Stephen's sisters were living there. Jenny was glad she wouldn't have to get into the lift too often; it looked even tinier than the one at Oak Hall. Stephen showed her the door between their rooms. 'That's the bathroom,' he said. Jenny just got a glimpse of disabled bars beside the toilet before Stephen hurried her on. 'And this is your room.'

The room was large, as big as the room she'd shared with Hayley at the home. The walls were decorated with pale yellow paper with tiny blue flowers that ended at a pine picture rail. The floor was wooden, with a large rug beside the bed. Jenny hoped she wouldn't keep tripping on it with her legs. The bed, wardrobe and dresser were pine too, and the yellow light that slanted in through the blinds on the large bay window made the room glow with a soft golden hue. Her bags had been brought in, and were sitting on the bed. There was a lamp and a clock on her bedside table, as well as a small vase of wild flowers.

'I picked you flowers in the garden with Mummy. Do you like the flowers, Jenny?'

Jenny walked into the room and sat on the bed. 'They're beautiful, Stephen. The whole room is beautiful.' She looked at the view of the garden through the window. She could hear birds singing, see the stream tumbling over rocks that may have been there naturally, or may have been added for effect. The house was truly beautiful, Stephen was sweet and nice, Helen and John seemed kind and loving, so Jenny wondered why she felt uneasy. Why her stomach was churning.

Just nerves, I guess, she told herself. It's just strange, to come here like this. To suddenly be part of someone else's family. What if they don't like me? What if I don't like them? What if they send me back, like Lee? It's normal to feel uneasy . . .

'Would you like a drink, Jenny?' Helen's voice called from the kitchen.

'Um, yes please.'

Jenny retraced her steps to the kitchen, following the direction the voice had come from to remind her of

49

the way. The house was long in the front, with two wings that jutted into the garden at the back. Her bedroom was in the east wing, and the kitchen was in the west wing. There were two doors leading out of the kitchen, one of which led out on to a patio in the garden. Jenny asked about the other door.

'That leads to my workshop,' Helen said. 'It's really the garage, but I've converted it. Do you want to see?'

Jenny did want to see, very much. 'Yes, please.'

'Well, have a drink first, and then I'll give you the tour. Okay?'

Jenny sipped cool lemonade at the big chunky kitchen table. Mr Holland – John – was also at the table, drinking coffee, and Stephen sat beside her on a chair with a plastic booster seat attached, making him high enough to reach the table. He swung his legs under him and tried to keep talking while he drank his juice, and ended up having a coughing fit and snorting juice out of his nose. Jenny patted his back and handed him a tissue. Helen came over, looking concerned. 'Are you all right, Stephen love?'

'Yes, Mummy, don't fret!'

A funny expression for a little boy, but then Stephen's use of language generally seemed very good for a child of his age.

When they'd finished their drinks, Helen, who had been wiping the counters, dried her hands on a tea towel and led the way into her workshop.

'Watch the step,' she said, holding Jenny's arm and helping her down.

The garage was like an Aladdin's cave. Its walls were lined with shelves laden with pots and plates, with figures and abstract pieces. The colours were earthy: blues and purples, greens and reds, but all deep and rich. Jenny stopped to stare at individual pieces. She barely remembered to draw breath, so taken was she by the beauty and excitement of what she was seeing. She lifted a plate, carefully holding the edges. It was painted with a swirling Celtic knot and rimmed with gold. Around the inside of the rim, dragons ran, each swallowing the tail of the one in front. She placed it back, and took up another piece. This was a dish, with a lid that sat flush on top. A sun was worked in relief on the lid, and painted orange and yellow, with a yellow knob in the centre to lift it. 'Your work is beautiful,' she whispered. Helen looked pleased, and thanked her.

'I know that *you're* very creative,' she said. 'I was hoping you could help me with my work?'

'Oh, I'd love to.'

Jenny still felt anxious, but now it was an anxiety tinged with excitement.

Could things be finally going her way?

Her eyes continued to scan the room. She saw a long wooden work table and beside it a large potter's wheel. She noticed that it was powered by a foot pedal. The sight reminded her once again of her disability. Helen saw her looking, and quickly said, 'Don't worry, I have a motorised one as well – I just prefer that one. Besides, there's lots of work to do that doesn't use the wheel: finishing and glazing and hand sculpting. Or I could teach you to make ocarinas.'

'Ocarinas?'

Stephen, who had been quiet until then, piped up with 'Can I show her, Mummy? Can I? Can I play Jenny my tunes?'

Stephen was standing by a table that at first seemed to be covered in large, shiny coloured pebbles. When Jenny looked more closely she saw that they were shaped more like flattened teardrops, with a mouth-piece at one end and holes on the top. Stephen picked one up, arranged his fingers over the holes and started to blow through the mouthpiece. Jenny expected a childish whistling noise to come out, but instead the garage was filled with a beautiful and eerie round-toned sound. The tune he played was familiar, although Jenny couldn't quite place it. Something by the Beatles maybe. Stephen played with a confidence and skill that was far beyond his years. He seemed lost in the music and Jenny felt that she might get lost in it too, as if time had stopped while she listened to him. When he fin-ished, Jenny and Helen applauded him and he gave a mock bow.

'Can I play another tune? I made up a new one, Mummy, did I tell you? Can I play it to you and Jenny? Can I?'

Jenny was leaning on her crutches and her arms were getting tired. She shifted her position and her crutch slipped on the dusty floor.

'Oh!' said Helen. 'Are you all right?' Jenny assured her that she was fine, but Helen still went over and held her arm. She then turned to Stephen and told him to pick out an ocarina for Jenny to keep. 'Then you can go and sit down in the garden and teach her how to play it,' she said.

Jenny took the smooth clay instrument that Stephen handed her. He had picked out one that was blue, with a purple and yellow butterfly painted on it. It just fitted into the palm of her hand. It had a loop at the opposite end from the mouthpiece, with a leather string threaded through it, so that Jenny could wear it around her neck like a pendant. 'Thank you,' she said, smiling at Stephen and then at Helen. 'I love it.'

Helen smiled at Jenny, and for a moment her smile wavered. She quickly brought the corners of her mouth back up, but Jenny couldn't help thinking that there was a strange, hungry look in her eyes.

Four

Jenny found she could make a pleasant enough sound with her ocarina even on her first attempt. Stephen taught her how to play a scale, and then he taught her *Twinkle Twinkle*. She was pleased with herself and played with the whistle as if she was a small child, trying to copy Stephen's way of vibrating his fingers to make the notes trill. He laughed at her attempts. 'You just have to practise,' he said when she sighed with frustration. 'You have to see the music in your head, and then your head tells your fingers what to do.' Jenny looked at Stephen, amazed at the maturity of his statement. He was lying on the grass looking at the sky. 'Mummy makes ones that look like birds as well,' he said. 'You put water in them and when you blow it sounds like birds singing. I like these ones better, though, because you can play tunes with them. I'm too little to make my own ocarina. When I'm bigger I'll make one. I'll make a yellow one that looks like the sunshine and a blue one that looks like night-time – if Mummy lets me make two – and I could give you one. Would you like one? Would you like the yellow one or the blue one?'

Jenny was going to answer, but Stephen didn't pause in his chattering long enough to give her a chance.

'That's if you don't go away, though. Lots of people go away. I hope you don't go, Jenny. I like you.'

Jenny thought he must have been thinking of the other children the Hollands had fostered, or maybe he was thinking of his sisters who died. Jenny wondered if he remembered his sisters, or if they died when he was a baby. He was still prattling on, telling her about how he broke his first ocarina by dropping it on the stone tiles in the kitchen, but Mummy didn't mind and made him another one. She decided not to ask him about his sisters. He probably didn't remember them, and if he did, she didn't want to upset him by talking about them. Instead she lay back, listening to the stream and the birds and Stephen's happy voice, and not realising that she was drifting off to sleep.

When she woke, Stephen had gone away and Mrs Holland was standing over her. 'Hello there, sleepy-head,' she said. Jenny rubbed her eyes and squinted through the evening sun.

'Oh, I must have gone to sleep.'

'Come on,' said Helen, 'I'll help you up. Dinner's ready.'

Jenny was starving. After the accident she had little interest in food. Maybe it was the depression, or maybe just being bedridden, but she just hadn't felt hungry. The hospital counsellor worried that she might be anorexic on top of everything, but her appetite had come back eventually.

The dinner was set up on the patio outside the kitchen. Pasta and sauce and salad and bread. Stephen was there already, and Mr Holland was bringing a jug of juice through from the kitchen.

Jenny leaned her crutches against the wall and smiled to hide how hard she had to concentrate to get to the table without them. She didn't always lean her weight on them even when she used them, but they gave her confidence. One step, two steps, she made it.

'This looks lovely,' she said, sliding herself into the seat.

If the Hollands had noticed her difficult steps, they didn't say, and the conversation around the table was light. Helen asked her about her ocarina playing.

'I'll need a lot of practice to be as good as Stephen,' she said, 'but I did manage to play *Twinkle Twinkle*.'

'Good for you,' Mr Holland said (John, Jenny reminded herself). John Holland was quieter than his wife and son. He hadn't said much to Jenny at all, just smiled and nodded occasionally. He was sipping wine and looking at Jenny. 'I do hope you'll be compatible.'

Helen shot him a look, and laughed and said, 'John, what a weird thing to say – compatible! He means he hopes you're happy with us, Jenny.'

'Thank you,' Jenny said, suddenly feeling shy and a little confused at John's choice of words.

They had ice-cream for dessert, which Stephen managed to spill all over himself. Helen went off to bath him and put him to bed, and Jenny, shy of being alone with John, excused herself and went to her room to unpack.

Her wheelchair was in her room, so she took off her legs and used that to move from her bed to the drawers, unpacking clothes and other bits and bobs. She didn't bother hanging anything in the wardrobe; it would have been too much effort to put her legs back on so that she could reach. In the bottom of the wardrobe she put Eve's box, after first running her fingers affectionately over its carved surface. The sound of beads rattling inside it was soothing, like a rain-stick, or like Eve's voice whispering to her.

She had several hardbacked notebooks that she used for writing down her poems, or sometimes drawings. She put most of them into the drawer in her bedside table, but the most recent one, which was only partially filled, she left on top of the table with a pen and a pencil beside it.

She had a photo of herself and her mum, standing in front of their old house, in a frame that her mum had made out of twisted metal with coloured glass gems worked into it. She stood it up beside the vase of flowers and looked at it for a moment. 'Look, mum,' she said out loud, 'I've got my own room in a big house, and a little brother. What do you think of that?'

She shivered then, and suddenly noticed that she was feeling chilly. She picked up a sweatshirt that she'd left on the bed and pulled it over her head. Then she swung herself out of the chair and on to the bed. She sat up, pushing pillows behind her until she was comfortable. Even sitting had felt funny at first – after the accident: her balance was all wrong – but she was used to it now.

She picked up her notebook and found a blank page to write on.

Happy

I remember the feeling.
It was yellow and warm.
It used to bubble and tickle
And make me laugh.
Will I feel it again?
What do I feel now?
Bubbling?
Or is it churning?
Burning?
Fear or hope?
I hope
I will be happy
Again.

She doodled around the edges of the poem. She drew the sun with rays coming out, the way a primary-school child might draw it. She drew butterflies and flowers, and on a new page she drew Stephen. She used the pencil to shape his face, smiling and looking as if he was about to speak. She shaded the contours of his cheeks, his eyebrows, his nose. When she was finished she looked at the drawing critically. The nose wasn't quite right, but on the whole she was pleased. It looked like Stephen.

She decided to write a poem about the little boy, and wrote the title:

But her pen stayed still and blotted the page as she thought about what to write. For some reason she thought of pan pipes, the breathy, mystical sound reminding her of Stephen's ocarina playing. Then her mind tumbled on to Peter Pan, the boy who never grew up. She supposed that if she left the Hollands after a few weeks or months, then Stephen would always be a little boy in her memory. Like Stephen's sisters would always be little girls in their parents' memories, and her own mother would always be young and pretty and vibrant in her mind. Eve would never grow to be an old woman now. 'Die young, stay pretty' – wasn't that a line from a song? Death steals potential. The potential to grow and the potential to grow old. But it wasn't better to die young. Jenny wanted to see her mother age and mature; she would have still loved her, she would have cared for her. And she didn't want Stephen just to be a little boy she knew once – she wanted someone to stay with her and grow old with her.

She had her pen in her mouth, staring at the page with just the one-word title, when there was a gentle knocking at her door. She quickly closed the book and called out, 'Come in.'

Helen came in carrying two steaming mugs. Jenny was instantly reminded of Lee, bringing her tea that day back at the home. She felt strong pangs of loneliness thinking about him, wondering what he was doing now.

Helen passed her a mug with little hearts around it, and kept one that said 'World's Best Mum' for herself. It wasn't tea in the mugs: it was cocoa, warm and milky. 'It'll help you sleep,' Helen said, sitting down on the end of Jenny's bed.

She smiled at Jenny and said, 'I know it must be difficult, settling in to a new place like this. I hope you're happy here with us.'

Jenny hoped so too, although she didn't say anything, just nodded. Then a thought struck her, and she spoke without really thinking.

'Did Lee sleep in this room?'

'Lee?'

'Lee Chan. You fostered him last year.'

'Oh, yes, Lee. He was a nice boy. Yes, actually he did have this room.'

Jenny felt a bit of a thrill, sleeping where Lee had slept. 'Why did you send him back?'

As soon as she'd said it, Jenny realised it sounded rude and wished she could take it back. At the same time, though, she wanted to know the answer.

Helen seemed flustered. 'Well, um, he just wasn't . . . that is, we . . . Well, it was the first time we'd fostered for a long . . . I mean, the first time we'd fostered at all, and we just needed a little more time before we were ready to take on someone long term. That's why. Are you and Lee friends?'

Jenny blushed and smiled, looking away.

'Oh,' said Helen, 'he's your boyfriend?'

'No! No, we're just friends, that's all.'

As Jenny sipped her cocoa she felt herself getting sleepy. 'I'm going to get ready for bed now,' she said. She was so sleepy that she didn't even remember Helen leaving, or putting on her nightdress, but she must have, because she was wearing it when she woke in the morning.

School was finished for the summer, but Jenny still had physio. The following day the ambulance came to the Hollands' house to take her to the hospital. The physiotherapists were pleased with her progress, and gave her some new, more difficult exercises to practise. During the session, Mr Evans came to talk to her. He said he'd been promised funding, and was working out the details of the skiing programme. He said she would get an appointment some time soon to be measured for special prosthetics that fitted into the adjusted skis. He spoke to the boy with the foot amputation as well, and for once he and Jenny acknowledged each other, exchanging excited smiles. All in all, the session went very well, and Jenny chatted happily to the ambulance crew as they drove her back home.

She scratched at an itch in the inside of her left elbow as the ambulance pulled up the driveway at the Hollands' house. She looked and noticed that there was a tiny red lump there. Probably an insect bite, she thought, I must have been bitten when I was sleeping on the grass yesterday.

Helen came out of the house wiping her hands on a cloth stained with reddish-brown clay. Her hair was wrapped in a bandana, and the clay-streaked smock she wore made her look like a 1970s hippie.

'I lost track of time,' she said. 'I was working on a new batch of ocarinas while Stephen had a nap. It takes concentration to get them just right. I meant to have some lunch ready for you.'

'Oh, don't worry,' Jenny said. 'I'm not that hungry anyway.' Jenny's tummy rumbled loudly enough to be heard by both of them, and they laughed.

'I'll rustle something up quickly. Just let me wash off this clay first.'

Jenny was tired after physio, and used her wheelchair to get into the house. Most of the doors had ramps rather than steps, and the corridors were wide and uncluttered, so getting around in a wheelchair was not too difficult. The interior doors of the house had even been widened to allow wheelchairs to get through more easily.

Jenny went straight to her room and opened the drawer in her bedside table. She riffled through the old notebooks until she found the one she wanted. She took it and her new one and put them in her lap along with a pen, then positioned her chair under the window. She was looking for a poem she remembered writing when she was getting ready for the ski trip with her old school. She flicked through the pages, and it was strange seeing the things that had troubled her then. Her nose was too big, or she'd argued with her friend. Things that seemed like the end of the world at the time. The world she had lived in where she never imagined life without legs, without her mother. Sometimes she felt old beyond her years. Like she'd lived a whole life's worth of troubles in two short years.

She found the poem. She'd doodled snowflakes around the edges of it.

I Wonder

I wonder if the world will blur,
And speed will carry me along.
If cold wind will enfold me,
Like the magic of an angel's song.
I wonder if I'll fly with joy,
While skiing will my heart be warm?
I wonder if I'll find myself,
And snow and cold will be my home.

She'd been really pleased with that poem. She showed it to her English teacher, who'd put a copy of it up on the wall of her classroom. She read it again and it stirred up the same feelings of excitement in her heart that it had over two years ago. More so now that speed was normally so elusive to her. She remembered reading it to Eve, and that memory brought with it fresh stabs of guilt and grief. But Eve had loved her poem. What was it she'd said? Jenny looked at the photo on her bedside table to try to jog her memory. That was it: she'd said she was proud to have a daughter who could express herself so artistically. Jenny gave the photo a wobbly-lipped smile and decided to copy the poem out into her new notebook, word for word, as if she'd written it now. She balanced her old notebook open in her lap, and then held open the new one with her left hand. With her right hand she fumbled for the pen, which had slid from her lap and was stuck down the side of the cushion in her chair. Her fingers got the pen, but as she lifted it, the cap caught on the zip of the cushion, causing the pen to catapult out of her hand and tumble end over end on to the floor beside the bed. What was worse, when the pen landed it rolled out of sight.

'Damn it!' she said under her breath, and wheeled her chair over to the bed. She couldn't see where the pen had got to, and wouldn't have been able to reach it if she had. She put the brake on her chair, and slid herself out of it and on to the floor. On her belly and her elbows, like a soldier might crawl through enemy lines, she pulled herself under the bed.

It was dusty and she sneezed. When she'd wiped her eyes, she saw the pen, flush against the wall at the far side of the bed. She went further in, and noticed a floorboard lift under her. She twisted around to look, and saw that where her elbow had pushed down on one end of a plank, the other end had lifted. She would have just ignored it, except that she saw something underneath the lifted board.

It would have been awkward for anyone to manoeuvre in the confined space under the bed, and for Jenny, with her fear of enclosed spaces and her lack of extra leverage from her legs, it took some time before she was able to look properly, and reach her hand into the gap. She was wary of spiders, but too curious to let that stop her. Her hands found several hard, flat rectangles, and she lifted them out one by one. Forgetting about her pen, she slid out backwards, holding the rectangles to her chest, and then leaned against the bed to look at them.

They were notebooks: hardbacks with plain covers, similar to the ones she wrote her poems in. On the front cover of each was written the same thing: 'Mandy's Diary – Top Secret'.

There were five notebooks altogether. Jenny examined each of them without opening them yet. She ordered them according to which looked the most battered and bent, putting the newest-looking one on the top. Who is Mandy? she wondered. She can't have been one of Stephen's sisters; they weren't old enough to keep diaries. It had to be either someone who lived in the house before the Hollands, or someone they'd fostered. She ran her hands over the cover of the newest book. 'Top Secret'. Should she open it? She'd be breaking the trust of Mandy, the girl who wrote the diaries. But Mandy was probably long gone. And if the diaries had been that important to her, she would have taken them with her, wouldn't she?

Unable to decide, she was startled by a knocking on her door.

'Just a minute,' she called, and without knowing why, she quickly hid the diaries, under her own notebooks in the drawer in the bedside table. The door opened as she was shutting the drawer. It was Stephen, looking tousle-haired after his nap.

"Lo, Jenny,' he said, 'Mummy's made some lunch.'

Jenny was still on the floor, so she pulled herself, with some difficulty, back up and into her chair.

Stephen had a small piece of blanket which he was holding up against his face with one hand while sucking the thumb of his other hand. Jenny had never seen him look so young. She let him sit on her lap as she wheeled herself to the family room beside the kitchen. When she got there, Helen's face fell when she saw Stephen slouched on Jenny's knee. 'What's the matter, love?' she said. 'Are you not feeling well?'

'Just sleepy, Mummy,' Stephen said.

Helen lifted him off Jenny and sat him down at the table. She felt his head, and the glands in his neck, which made him giggle as it tickled him. 'Well, you don't have a fever,' she said, as if she was talking to herself. 'That's good.' She almost imperceptibly lifted the sleeve of his T-shirt and looked at the top of his arm. She dropped it again as if satisfied, and then smiled at Jenny. 'There's soup, and fresh bread. Both from the freezer, I'm afraid, but still good, I think.'

The food smelt delicious, and Jenny was hungry. As they ate, Stephen perked up a bit, and Helen seemed to relax more as he did. She asked Jenny about physio, and Jenny told her about the proposed skiing trip.

'Wow!' she said, 'that's exciting! I used to ski when I was younger. It's a wonderful feeling.'

'Can I go skiing, Mummy?' Stephen asked.

'Maybe when you're bigger,' said Helen.

'When am I going to get bigger?' Stephen whined plaintively. 'It's taking too long!'

'You, young man,' said Helen, trying to tame his wild hair with her hands, 'need to stop worrying about getting bigger, and enjoy being as big as you are. This is the best time of your life. You're big enough to play and learn new things, but small enough for cuddles and naps. Lots of adults wish they could say that.'

'Okay, Mummy.' Stephen laid his head down on the table and played with his piece of bread.

'Still tired, love?'

'Mmm.'

Helen lifted Stephen down from his chair and laid him on the little two-seater sofa that stood against one wall of the family room. She took the throw that was folded over the top of the sofa, and gently laid it over him. Jenny saw the worry in her eyes, and wondered if she thought he might be getting ill like his sisters.

After they'd finished eating, Jenny said, 'I'll watch him if you want to get back to your workshop. I've got a book to read.'

'Oh, well, if you don't mind, Jenny. I do have some things I want to finish up. Thank you.'

Jenny went quickly to her room and opened her drawer. She looked again at the diaries, and after a little thought, selected the oldest-looking one, and popped it into her chair, as well as a copy of *Anne of Green Gables*, in case Helen asked her what she was reading. She brought them back to the kitchen and settled herself beside Stephen. Helen assured her she would come if called, and then headed off into her workshop.

Jenny waited until the shuffling noises from the

workshop settled down into a steady rhythm before she took out the diary. She didn't know why she was being so secretive, but somehow she wanted to keep her discovery to herself.

Holding the book in her hands, she paused for a few heartbeats, then took a deep breath and opened it.

Five

On the inside cover was written:

This is the diary of
Amanda Jean Patterson
186 Aldergrove Terrace,
Worthing
Aged ten years

Across the page was the first entry in the diary:

Tuesday 19th December

Today was my tenth birthday. I had a party at
my house and seven girls from my class at school
came to it. We had sandwiches and cakes and
crisps and sausages and fizzy drinks. I got a
Famous Five book, some nail varnish, a pink top, a
hairbrush and mirror set, a pair of roller skates
and a record (Diana Ross). But my favourite
present was from my best friend Alison, and it is
this book. She says she has one and she uses it
as a diary and she writes about what she's
done every day in it and wouldn't it be fun if I

69

did the same thing and we could read each other's. She gave me different coloured pens too and I will write in a different colour every day.

Mum didn't shout at the party, except afterwards she got cross because of the mess, but I quickly tidied it up and then she was happy again. Tomorrow we're going to visit Dad in prison and I will show him the cards I got for my birthday. By the time I'm eleven, Dad will be back home again with me and Mum. I can't wait for things to be the way they used to be.

So, Mandy's dad was in prison, Jenny thought. I suppose that figures, if she ended up getting fostered. It was not unusual for children who came through Oak Hall to have one or more parents in prison. They usually didn't want to talk about it if they did, though. Jenny wondered if Mandy had been at Oak Hall. She'd only been there a year and a half, so Mandy could have left before she came. Probably not, though – Mr and Mrs Holland would surely not have fostered so soon after their daughters died. Stephen was only five, so the daughters must have died within the last four years or so. Besides, Helen had said that Lee was the first child they'd fostered.

Jenny read on through the diary, skimming the bits she found boring. There was a lot about Mandy's friend Alison, and things about what she'd done at school, and how well she'd done in spelling tests and stuff like that. The same kind of things that Jenny would have written about when she was ten. Sometimes Mandy talked about her mum getting angry with her, or crying. Jenny stopped and read over one page:

Tuesday 15th May

Today Mum hit me again. I was playing catch with Alison in the garden. We were running about and making lots of noise, and Mum was there hanging out washing. Mum told us to be quiet, and we tried to, but then we forgot and we were noisy again. Mum shouted and told us we had to go inside. We were still running about inside and I accidentally knocked over the clothes that Mum had been ironing. Alison stood on Mum's white blouse and put a muddy foot-print on it. When Mum came in she got really mad. She shouted at us and told Alison to go home, and then she slapped me hard on my face. My face is still red where she hit me. I said I was sorry about the ironing, and then Mum said she was sorry about hitting me, and then we had a hug, and I helped Mum to fold up the clothes again.

Jenny stopped reading and thought about her own mum. She tried to remember if Eve had ever hit her. She thought she had sometimes smacked her hand or leg, when she was tiny. She didn't remember her ever slapping her face, though, or hitting her at all when she was as old as ten. The thought of her mum made tears form in her eyes and roll down her cheeks. She didn't notice the tears until one fell on the page she was looking at. She blotted it with the edge of her T-shirt, not wanting to smudge the writing. Eve's voice was echoing in her mind.

'Don't cry, sweetie, it doesn't matter.'

She remembered when she'd heard those words. She'd been playing in the house, running about like Mandy had been. Her mum had been sitting on the floor, with her legs under a low coffee table. She had her case of beads open, with little compartments that had different beads and clasps and things in them. Some of the beads her and her mum had made out of coloured clay, some Eve had bought or traded. Jenny remembered saying, 'Look at me, Mummy Evie, I can do a cartwheel!' and before Eve could tell her to be careful, she'd launched herself on to her hands and crashed into the table. The case of beads had pitched into the air and glass and clay and metal and plastic had tumbled out, like a rainbow-coloured fountain. Jenny had slumped on to the floor, sore from bumping into the table and horrified at the mess she'd made. She must only have been about six or seven. Eve had taken her and hugged her and sat her on her knee. 'Look,' she'd said, pointing at the beads that glinted on the floor. 'Our carpet is the sky over Greece, and the beads are all the twinkly stars that Mummy Eve saw. But you know what, Jenny? These stars are special because they are lots of colours, and for every star you pick up and put back in Mummy's box, you get to make a wish.'

72

Jenny still remembered crawling around the floor finding stars and making wishes. She couldn't remember what she'd wished for, probably sweets or ice-cream or something like that, but she remembered how happy she'd felt. She guessed that Eve wasn't always so patient with her, but that one memory stood out. Eve, smiling, surrounded by beads.

'Did you hurt yourself, Jenny?'

Stephen had woken up and must have noticed the tears on Jenny's cheeks. She quickly wiped them away and smiled at the little boy. 'No, I didn't hurt myself; I was just reading a sad story.' She showed him her *Anne of Green Gables* book.

'I can read!' Stephen said. 'Mummy taught me. I like *The Wishing Chair*, by Enid Blyton. Maybe your chair's a wishing chair, Jenny. What would you wish for if it was, Jenny? I'd wish I was bigger. Or that I could eat ice-cream all the time. What would you wish for, Jenny?'

Jenny would have wished to turn back time, of course, to make things different. But she didn't say that; instead she said, 'Well, I think I'd wish that you really were my brother, and that I could eat ice-cream all the time too!'

Stephen laughed, delighted by her answer.

'Where's Mummy?' he asked.

'She's in her workshop. Do you want me to get her?'

Stephen thought for a while. 'No, it's okay,' he said. 'You and me can do stuff. Mummy doesn't like to be disturbed while she's working.'

'Maybe I should tell her you're awake, though,' Jenny said, remembering Helen's concern over Stephen's sleepiness.

'Okay, if you want.'

Jenny went over and opened the door to Helen's workshop. She called out as she went in, carefully dropping her chair down the single step. There was no sign of Helen. As Jenny wondered where she could be, she noticed for the first time a door on the opposite side of the garage. The door was open slightly, and light spilled out of it into the room.

Jenny went back into the kitchen and said to Stephen, 'She's not in there, but there's a door open on the other side.'

'She must be in the underground room,' Stephen said. 'I'm not allowed in there because of the hot hot oven.'

Oh, Jenny thought, there must be a kiln down in a cellar or something. Right enough, she didn't remember seeing a kiln in the garage. She went back into the workshop and over to the open door. Stairs led down from it, turning a corner so that Jenny couldn't see into the cellar. Of course Jenny couldn't go down stairs in her chair, and stairs were very difficult with her legs as well. She was about to call Helen when she heard her voice. It sounded as though she was talking to someone, like the one-sided conversation of someone on a telephone.

'Yes, lethargy, he's very sleepy.

'No, I checked the injection site and there's no inflammation, and he doesn't seem to have a fever.

74

'Yes, you're right: it could be a good sign. We should get Dr Jo to come and look at him all the same.

'I know, her tests looked promising, but I'm trying not to get too hopeful.

'No, I haven't got around to running the gel yet. I've got the samples ready though.

'Yeah, we'll know more tomorrow.

'Yeah.

'Yeah.

'Okay, love, we'll talk more later.

'Oh, would you get milk on the way home?

'Thanks, love, see you later.'

Jenny didn't move, trying to think about what she'd just heard. Injection site? Was Stephen getting treatment? That was fair enough, she supposed; maybe he needed treatment to prevent him from getting whatever illness his sisters had. There was no reason why Helen and John should have discussed that with her. But who were they talking about when they said, '*Her* tests look promising'?

Just then she heard Helen's footsteps coming up the stairs.

Jenny wheeled her chair backwards, as quickly as she could. By the time Helen reached the top of the stairs, Jenny was back at the door, and started wheeling forwards, as if she'd just come in.

'Hello, Jenny,' Helen said, smiling. 'Did you want something, love?'

'I just came to tell you that Stephen woke up.'

'He did? Good. I'll come and check on him.'

Helen followed her back into the kitchen, where Stephen was helping himself to a drink of juice. He was standing on a chair that he'd pulled over to the sink, and holding his cup of orange concentrate under the running tap.

'I'll get that for you, pet,' Helen said, taking the cup from him.

'I can do it, Mummy!'

Jenny noticed that Helen's hands looked very clean, with faint white lines, as if she'd rubbed powder in them that had got stuck in the little creases of her skin. They reminded her of something.

'Were you firing some pieces?' she asked her.

'Hmm?'

'Stephen said the kiln was down in the cellar. I saw you coming up the stairs.'

'Oh, yes. A batch of plates. A couple of them had got a bit out of shape, but I decided to fire them anyway, so you could practise painting them. That way if you mess up, it doesn't matter, and if you produce a masterpiece, we can market it as having a unique hand-made, non-uniform shape.'

Jenny laughed. 'You know all the tricks,' she said.

'Well, I've been doing it for a long time now.'

While Helen was talking, Stephen had taken his cup back from her hand and filled it with water. Jenny gave him a conspiratorial wink, as he drank some juice.

Jenny was wearing her ocarina around her neck, and she asked Stephen if he felt awake enough to give her another lesson.

'Oh, okay,' he said, 'but only if you promise to play cars with me afterwards.'

Jenny had no brother or sisters, and when she'd had friends around to play she didn't remember ever playing cars with them. She'd had a car for her Barbie, but she didn't really play with it, just sat it on her shelf, where it looked nice.

'How about you teach me another tune, and then I watch you play cars? Would that do?'

'Yeah!'

Stephen seemed much better now, and back to his usual bouncy self. He ran off in the direction of his bedroom, and came back minutes later with his ocarina around his neck and carrying an armful of toy cars.

'Do you mind if I get back to work?' Helen said. 'I've got some things I want to get done.'

'Sure,' said Jenny. She watched Helen as she went through the door to the workshop. Was she going to make some more ceramics, or was she going to 'run some tests'? Jenny wished she could go down the stairs to the cellar and see what was down there. Was it just a kiln, or was there something else?

She shook her head and told herself to stop being silly. The problem with only hearing half a conversation was that you could get completely the wrong idea of what was being said. For all she knew, Helen and John might have been discussing some TV show or something.

'Jenny, *come on!*'

Stephen had been trying to attract her attention and was hopping about in frustration.

'All right, Mr Impatient,' said Jenny. 'I'm coming.'

Once again Jenny was entranced by Stephen's ocarina playing. The simple flute had only six holes, and yet by partially covering holes, or by altering the strength of his breath, he could produce a wide range of sounds.

Stephen taught her a tune that he said was the theme tune to an old cowboy film. Once she'd mastered the tune, or at least the basics of it – her playing didn't have any of the subtleties of Stephen's – she released Stephen from his role as teacher, and watched him crawl around the floor, racing his cars and giving an endless running commentary. After an eight-car pile-up, he sat back, cross-legged and said, 'I've got to go to day care tomorrow. Mummy home-schools me some days and some days I go to day care. I've had a holiday from school because of you coming, but I have to go back now.'

'Do you?' said Jenny. 'What do you do at day care?'

'We do sand and dough and outdoor play and snack time and story time and imaginative play and construction toys and singing and dressing up and painting and junk art and nap time and reading corner and jigsaws and . . . um, some other stuff, I can't remember.'

'Oh my goodness!' said Jenny, 'that sounds like lots of fun. Do you like it?'

'Um . . .' Stephen considered his answer, chewing his lip and staring off into space. 'Yes, I do like it. It's better than handwriting that I have to do with Mummy. But it's not as good as science and history, because I like to learn about things, and some of the children at day care are a bit silly and they don't know how to read or anything. I liked the day care I went to before this one better, and the one that my friend Johnny went to – that was a long time ago, I can't really remember it so well.'

Jenny thought that to a little child even a few weeks or months must seem like a long time. 'What happened to Johnny?' she asked.

'He went away,' Stephen said sadly. 'All my friends do. I think he went to big-boy school.'

'Does he still come and visit?'

'He did at first, but not any more.'

'Well, never mind, you'll make new friends.'

'Yeah. Suppose. Except Mummy doesn't let me have friends round to the house any more. She says it's better that way.'

Jenny wondered why Helen didn't want Stephen's friend to visit, but she didn't ask him about it. She tried to distract the little boy from his sadness and said, 'I bet the red car is faster than the green car.'

'No, it's not!' said Stephen, suddenly happy again. 'The green car is super fast. Look, it's faster than a speeding bullet.' He slipped happily back into his car-racing game, and Jenny indulgently listened to his imaginative descriptions of the cars and their drivers. She liked listening to him, but was nevertheless looking forward to a few hours without him the next day. Much as she loved him, it would be nice to get a bit of peace.

John came home with the milk that he'd promised, as well as a box with a label that said 'Biohazard'. He saw Jenny looking at it worriedly and laughed.

'Don't worry,' he said. 'I just used an empty box from work to bring home some paperwork. Nothing dangerous.'

Jenny smiled and nodded, but as John lifted the box past her, she thought she heard a clink from inside it, like glass bottles rattling together. She tried not to look alarmed, as if she hadn't heard anything. But her mind was working overtime. Why would he lie and say the box contained paperwork if it actually contained glass bottles? What had he brought home from the lab, and did it have anything to do with Helen 'running tests'?

After dinner Jenny asked if she could phone Oak Hall and speak to Hayley. John and Helen said that was fine, and brought her a cordless phone, which she took into her room.

Sarah answered the phone, and sounded genuinely pleased to hear Jenny's voice. She asked her how she was and how she was settling in. Jenny said she was well and the family were very nice. She didn't mention her worries about Helen's phone conversation or John's box of biohazards. She was probably just being paranoid, and if she mentioned it to Sarah, it would only cause a lot of fuss and she'd end up being embarrassed, or worse, sent back to Oak Hall.

Sarah fetched Hayley, who was very excited to speak to her. Jenny had to hold the phone a few inches from her ear to avoid being blasted by Hayley's loud, enthusiastic voice. She was going out to her foster home in a few days. She'd been with the family for an outing already. They'd taken her to the cinema and for ice-cream. Even if Jenny had wanted to tell Hayley about the mysterious phone call or the box of biohazards, she would hardly have had a chance: it was so difficult for her to get a word into the conversation. It seemed too silly anyway, to say anything. Nothing had happened. She was just picking up on tiny things that probably meant nothing. She told Hayley about the diaries, though.

'That's so cool,' said Hayley, 'but guess what? I'm going to have a TV in my room and cable and everything.'

Jenny gave up, and after telling Hayley that she missed her, and that she was sure she'd be really happy in her foster home, she hung up.

She wondered about ringing Lee, but realised she didn't have his phone number at his foster home. She didn't want to ring Oak Hall again and ask for it; that would be too embarrassing. In the end she decided to write him a letter. He'd given her his address when he'd come to visit that day, on a scrap of paper, and luckily she'd remembered to copy it on to the inside cover of her notebook.

She had some writing paper and envelopes in her drawer; Sarah had given them to her as a leaving gift. The paper was blue with faint clouds in the background. Jenny went and asked Helen what the postal address of their house was so she could write it at the top of her letter. Helen looked almost startled when she asked, although Jenny couldn't imagine why.

'We don't get any post delivered here,' she said. 'We use a post office box in Worthing. I'll give you the box number and address of the post office.'

'You don't get any post?' Jenny asked, confused. 'Why not?'

'Oh,' said Helen, with a smile that looked a little forced, 'we like being secluded here, in our own little world. We don't want people calling round to the house all the time.'

'But the postman doesn't come in or anything . . .' Jenny went on.

'Jenny!' Helen cut across her words and her voice was raised, causing John to look up from the newspaper he was reading. She cleared her throat and lowered her voice again. 'It's just easier this way. I get a lot of deliveries with my business. It's easier if they all come into the post office box.' She smiled, then looked down at her own newspaper, signalling the end of the discussion.

Jenny went back to her room, feeling slightly confused. She wrote the PO box number in the top right corner of her writing paper, and the phone number of the Hollands underneath it. She hoped that Lee would take the hint and ring her up.

Dear Lee

What should she write? Jenny wanted to write 'I love you, I love you, I love you', but of course she didn't. In the end her letter was friendly and chatty. She told him about what she'd been doing at the Hollands' house, and talked about Stephen. She told him about her ocarina lessons, and how she couldn't wait to do some work in Helen's workshop.

She asked about him, and told him what Hayley had

told her about her new foster family, as well as some news from Oak Hall.

In the end she signed off:

Miss you, Jenny xxx

She kissed the paper, and sighed as she slipped it into the envelope.

Six

Helen brought her cocoa again at bedtime, and again she was asleep before she realised it.

The next morning breakfast was a bit rushed as Helen got Stephen ready for day care. She said she was going to do a bit of shopping after she dropped him off, and asked Jenny if she needed anything. For one horrible moment Jenny thought she was going to have to ask Helen to buy her sanitary towels. She knew her period was due soon, and wasn't sure if she had enough. Then, with a cool rush of relief, she remembered unpacking a full packet.

'No thanks,' she said, 'I'm fine.'

She'd got used to embarrassing things at the hospital, having to be lifted on to the bedpan, and later the toilet. Having to be given sponge baths, feeling like a baby having its nappy changed. The nurses were very good: they would chat to Jenny as if they were just taking her blood pressure or something, and she did get used to it. The first time she got her period in the hospital the nurse asked her if she'd ever had periods before.

'Yes,' she'd said quietly.

84

She had had a period before, before the accident. Eve had noticed Jenny's body beginning to show signs of changing from a child's to a woman's. She'd given Jenny a big talk about the joys of womanhood, and how it brought your body into harmony with mother earth and the moon goddess. Jenny just smiled and nodded; she knew it made Eve happy to talk like that. But when Eve suggested they do a ritual that involved dancing barefoot on a hill in the moonlight on the first night of her first period, Jenny was mortified. So when it did happen, she kept it secret from Eve.

She already helped with the laundry, so it was easy enough for her to deal with soiled underwear, and she went and bought herself what she needed from the chemist. She felt kind of guilty, spoiling the moment Eve had planned, but there was no way she was going to dance on a hill so that any other mad hippie passing by would know what was happening to her.

It only happened once anyway, before the accident.

'When I get back,' Helen said, 'you can come and help me in the workshop if you like.'

'Great!'

John had already left for work, so when Helen and Stephen left, Jenny had the house to herself. It suddenly struck her that she hadn't been alone in a house since before the accident. There was always someone at her hospital, and at Oak Hall as well, so it felt strange being alone, but in a good way. As if she was reclaiming a little of her independence.

She decided to have another look at Mandy's diaries.

She took them from her drawer, and lay down on her bed to read them.

She started on the second diary this time. It began with Mandy's eleventh birthday.

Wednesday 19th December

Dad has been home from prison for two weeks now. I don't like having him home and I wish he would go back to prison. He drinks too much and shouts and he thinks he can order me around even though he's hardly seen me for more than two years. Yesterday I was just minding my own business, watching cartoons, and Dad comes in and starts yelling about the 'bloody mess' and the 'bloody noise' and can't a man get any peace in his own 'bloody house'. It's just as much my 'bloody house' as it is his. And Mum sticks up for him. It's not fair! It's like nobody cares about me any more. I hate them.

Jenny tried to picture Mandy as she read her words. Was she tall or short? Pretty or plain? For some reason she formed a picture of her in her mind that looked like Little Orphan Annie, all red curly hair and freckles. She's probably nothing like that, she thought, but still the image persisted. The Mandy in her mind was shaking her finger and stamping her foot crossly.

She flicked through a few more pages, and then read on:

I can hear Mum and Dad fighting downstairs. I
know what it's about. The same thing they've
been fighting about for the last two weeks.
'When are you gonna get off your bum and get a
job?' (except Mum didn't say 'bum' – she said a
much ruder word) 'Who's gonna give me a job
with a criminal record?' 'Blah, blah, blah, blah,
blah!' Talking of records, I wish they would put
on a new one. Ha ha. I wanted to have Alison
round for a sleepover, I've been asking for ages,
and Mum always says, 'Next week, love, okay?'
But then next week comes and she still says no.
It's not fair! I asked her why not, and she said,
'It's best not to annoy your dad, you know what
he's like with his moods.' Yeah, I know what he's
like – he's like a big fat pain in the bum!

Mandy had drawn a picture of a bottom with lines
coming off it as if it was hurting. Jenny laughed at the
sight of it.

She read on for a while, sometimes flicking pages,
sometimes getting engrossed and reading days at a time.

A lot of entries were about a boy in her class called
Peter Welshman.

'. . . Peter's got gorgeous brown eyes . . .'
    '. . . I noticed today how artistic Peter's
hands are . . .'
        '. . . I bet Peter's really strong and athletic. I

saw him across the field in PE, the boys were doing football while we were doing hockey. His legs are really muscley and he was running really fast . . .'

From the way she described him, he sounded like some sort of all-round wonderful guy: clever, funny, handsome, sporty. She hadn't actually ever spoken to him, though, not directly anyway. The closest she'd come was through two other people:

'. . . I asked Alison to ask John Browne to ask Peter if he's done his maths homework and would he tell me what he got for question number seven. John Browne came back and told Alison that Peter said, yes, and he got 36!'

Mandy had drawn little thirty-sixes in hearts all around the edges of the page.

'Get a grip of yourself, girl,' Jenny told the diary.

It was funny reading Mandy's diary. Jenny was already starting to think of her as a friend. It was rare for Jenny to find a new friend who didn't see her chair, who didn't pretend not to look at her legs, who didn't judge her or expect anything from her. She liked being talked to like a normal person, even if it was only through words in a diary.

Jenny wondered if they would ever meet. Where was Mandy now?

She heard the sound of Helen's car pulling into the driveway, and once again hid the diaries away.

'Hi, Helen, can I help you in with the shopping?'

Helen was bent over the boot of the car and jumped when Jenny spoke to her, narrowly avoiding banging her head.

'Oh, I didn't hear you coming! Hi, yes, thank you.'

She lifted a couple of bags of groceries out of the boot and passed them to Jenny. Was it just her imagination, or did Jenny notice her hide something in the corner behind some bags? She told herself to stop being so paranoid – she was probably just rearranging things to give her bags that weren't too heavy or something like that. She went in and through to the kitchen, balancing the bags on her knee. Helen came behind her and put her shopping on the kitchen table.

'Stephen didn't stop talking about you all the way to day care,' she said. 'He's very fond of you. John and I couldn't have any more children after, um, after Stephen, and we didn't want him to be an only child.'

She seemed a little flustered and Jenny guessed the loss of her girls must still lie heavily on her mind. Of course it would.

'I'm very fond of him too,' Jenny said. 'I didn't have any brothers or sisters myself. Except in the home, where there's lots of other kids, y'know, but, um, yeah, he's lovely.'

Jenny felt a little awkward, and was glad when Helen said, 'Well, I haven't forgotten that I promised to let you work on some pots today. Are you still up for it?'

'Yeah, I can't wait.'

They went into the workshop, where a second potter's

wheel now stood beside the foot-operated one.

'I got John to bring that down from the attic for you,' Helen said, seeing her looking at it. She got Jenny a sort of apron with sleeves, the kind of thing you sometimes get to wear at the hairdressers, and then she pulled a lump of clay out of a big sack and handed half of it to her.

'It's amazing stuff,' she said, smoothing her own lump of clay, after dipping her hands into a bowl of water and wetting it slightly. 'Like this, it's just a brown lump, dug up from the earth, but it holds so much possibility. This lump could become a plate, or a cup, or a beautiful fig-ure, or even an ocarina, making music. It says in the Bible that God made man from clay from the earth. Look at it, Jenny, does it look like flesh? No! It looks like a brown lump, but look what it can become.' She indicated the shelves full of her work. 'Did you know that ceramics can be used to make body armour? And that some ceramics are used in electrical circuits? Even tiles on space rockets. So many possibilities.'

She seemed almost reverent in the way she handled the clay, and Jenny stared at her, entranced. She watched Helen's hands caressing the clay and imagined God forming man. Was her mastery over clay a way for Helen to feel in control? The bereavement counsellor had talked about the panic some people feel when they lose someone, because there was nothing they could do to stop it. Had Helen felt that when she lost her daughters? That she should have saved them but couldn't.

Helen placed her lump on the centre of her wheel, and indicated for Jenny to do likewise.

'It's very important that it's exactly in the centre,' she said, adjusting Jenny's slightly. 'Now wet your hands.' Jenny dipped her hands into a bowl of water that was already tinged with some reddish-brown particles, and wrapped them around her lump of clay. Helen started her wheel, and told her just to feel the clay turning in her hands to begin with.

It felt strange: cold and solid, yet malleable, yielding under her hands. Jenny felt the excitement of what Helen had been saying. The clay held so many possibilities. What would hers become?

'Now, use your thumbs to put pressure on the top of the clay, gradually hollowing out the inside. See? It's becoming a pot.'

Jenny grinned, thrilled that her clay did look nearly like a pot already.

'Now you get to be creative,' Helen said. 'You can make it short and wide, or tall and thin. Play with it – if you mess it up, you can just scrunch it up and start again.'

Jenny did play, making her pot taller and then wider, giving it ripples and then smoothing it out again. She tried making a wide rim that curved outwards; she pulled the clay between her fingers, feeling like a master craftsman with a perfect touch. Then suddenly the whole pot crumpled and the lopsidedness of it made it fly off the centre of the wheel. Jenny and Helen both laughed.

'Try again,' Helen said. 'Only this time visualise what you want your pot to look like before you start. Hold the image in your mind, and let your hands form it. After your pot has partially set, you could add trimmings or etchings.' She showed Jenny some pots that had additional bits of clay added to their outsides, or patterns imprinted on their curved walls.

Jenny watched Helen demonstrate some techniques with tools and moulds. Her mind was awhirl with ideas for her own pot. Would she try and keep it simple, or would she be adventurous and go for something elaborate? She looked around the room at all the pieces Helen had made.

Jenny wanted to try everything. She asked Helen to pass her a jug from the shelf and asked if she would mind if she copied it.

'Not at all,' said Helen. 'Imitation is the sincerest form of flattery.'

The jug was about a foot tall, with a pouring spout and a swan-neck handle. Twisted cables of clay hugged its contours from top to bottom, and between them diamonds were etched with pieces of mirror glinting from their recessed centres. The jug was painted shades of pink and purple and blue that merged together, adding to the effect of its shaping. The interior was painted dark midnight blue, and looking into it was like looking into a mysterious underwater lake, or the depths of the night sky.

'Well, you're certainly ambitious!' Helen said, laughing. 'And why not?'

She began explaining to Jenny about how to form the jug shape, using a large lump of clay and starting with it quite tall and narrow, then putting her arm inside it and guiding the bottom part out to form the rounded base. Helen started it off, and then Jenny tried to use a tool called a jogger to smooth the outside of the bowl-shaped part of the jug – but each time she tried, she pushed it through the edge of the clay, making the whole thing collapse. She sighed with frustration, and Helen said, 'Don't worry, you're doing really well. It just takes practice.' She held her hands over Jenny's and with her help Jenny managed to finish shaping the piece. She was very careful when it came to making the rim, remembering what happened to her first attempt. Helen showed her how to pinch out a spout, pausing the wheel's movement as she did. When the basic shape was finished, they turned off the wheel and admired it.

Except for the lack of handle, it looked like a jug. Of course the twiddly bits would have to be added later, when the clay had firmed up a bit, and she couldn't have done it without Helen's help, but Jenny was incredibly pleased with the jug nevertheless.

She sat staring at it, without being able to stop herself from grinning.

'See,' said Helen, 'you have a natural talent. You never know what potential is in you until you try.'

They put Jenny's jug aside to dry and Helen showed her some painting techniques. The time passed quickly, and before they realised it, it was time for Helen to go and collect Stephen from day care. They'd worked right through lunchtime, and Jenny offered to make some sandwiches while Helen was out.

'Oh thanks, that would be lovely,' Helen said. 'Use whatever you want from the fridge, and the bread bin is over by the microwave.'

They washed their hands in a sink in the workshop, and left the aprons hanging up by the door. Jenny went to get her legs, figuring that using them would be easier than manoeuvring around the kitchen in her chair. She thought of all the times the care workers had given her a hard time about HE, and here she was volunteering to prepare food.

Making her jug had made her feel confident, though, as if she could do anything. When she sat at the potter's wheel, it didn't matter that she had no legs. She had used the talent in her hands and her mind, and she'd done as well as anyone could. She even sang to herself as she pottered around the kitchen, finding tomatoes and ham and cheese and bread and butter, and feeling like she owned the world.

She worked quite slowly. Although making sandwiches was hardly a complicated task, it was the first food Jenny had prepared in ages and even simple things like buttering the bread didn't come easily to her. She stood at the counter to begin with, but balancing while standing still was more difficult than walking and she soon got tired. She sat down at the table to rest while she sliced the tomatoes, and then walked over to the waste bin to scrape in the ends. Something in the bin caught her eye and she leaned over to have a closer look, steadying herself on the counter with her hand. Peeping out from under some other rubbish she saw something she'd seen countless times in the hospital: white latex surgical gloves. She stared at them, wondering what they were doing there, and then she remembered Helen's hands. The other day, when Stephen hadn't been feeling well and she'd called Helen up from the underground room where the kiln is, she saw white lines on Helen's hand while she washed them and they'd reminded her of something. Now she knew what it was. The insides of latex gloves have a layer of powder, so that the gloves don't stick. When she'd seen nurses or doctors take off their gloves, their hands would be covered in the same sort of white powder. So Helen wore surgical gloves to put things into the kiln? That didn't make sense. The gloves were too thin to protect her hands from the heat. She thought about that for a while, and then realised that Helen would be back soon and she hadn't finished making the sandwiches yet.

She got back to work, and was just about to cut through the rounds of bread with a large knife when Stephen burst into the kitchen and ran over and hugged her legs.

Jenny's balance was lost and her arms instinctively shot upward. The knife she'd been holding flew into the air, and although she could see it spinning, about to fall where Stephen stood, she was unable to balance herself to stop it.

'Move!' she shouted, just as Helen came in and took in the scene.

Helen dashed at Stephen and pulled him away. The knife clattered on to the kitchen floor. The look that Helen flashed at Jenny made her freeze with shock. She looked angry and vicious, as if she might strike out at her.

'I'm sorry.' Jenny's voice came out shaky with an impending sob. 'I was cutting the sandwiches, and Stephen ran in, and I lost my balance. I'm sorry.'

She was clutching the counter, her legs sticking out at strange angles.

Helen immediately smiled, although her mouth twitched as she did so, as if it was an effort for her to form the expression. 'Of course. Here, let me help you.'

She took Jenny's arm and helped her to straighten up. 'I get a bit over-protective of Stephen sometimes, because – well, because he's so precious. But there's no harm done. Just a little accident. You sit down, I'll finish these. They look lovely, thank you.'

Helen was talking too fast, and Jenny felt upset and anxious. She could feel her heart beating in her chest. She'd felt so good, making a pot and then making lunch, but a tiny thing like Stephen running over to her had made her practically throw a knife at him. Maybe she shouldn't even try to do things like normal people, maybe she should just accept being disabled. Her mood had plummeted.

Stephen didn't seem to have picked up on the atmosphere: he sat beside Jenny and started telling her about what he'd done all day at day care. She only half listened, and at the same time watched Helen's back as she finished the sandwiches and made drinks.

By the time Stephen had finished speaking, Helen had brought over the food. She looked calmer, and her smile seemed more genuine, as she told Stephen about the pot that Jenny had made.

'When I grow up I want to be a potter and a scientist just like my Mummy,' Stephen said, as he nibbled at a sandwich. He'd wanted to join in with the late lunch, even though he'd already eaten at day care and obviously wasn't really hungry. When Helen and Jenny had finished, Helen took away all three plates and brought over some fruit. Jenny was eating grapes when the phone rang.

It was Sarah from Oak Hall, telling her she had an appointment before her next physio session to get her new legs fitted, and that the ambulance would come for her an hour early.

Wow, she'd been waiting to hear about her new legs, the ones that would fit into special skis. Had it not been for the incident with the knife, she'd have been thrilled. As it was, she didn't know how she felt. Happy or sad? Hopeful or pessimistic?

Tired.

She suddenly felt very tired, and homesick for Oak Hall, and homesick for her mum. She didn't want to live with strange people who might be hiding things from her. She didn't want to have no family of her own. Or no legs of her own.

It wasn't fair.

'If you don't mind, I'm going to go and have a nap,' she said.

Stephen started to complain, but Helen shushed him

with promises of pushing him on his swing. Jenny got her crutches and walked slowly to her room.

She lay on her bed and read a book, and actually did doze off. She slept until she was woken later in the afternoon by the doorbell ringing.

She got up to go to the toilet and when she opened the door to her room, she heard Helen's voice saying, 'Jo! It's good of you to come so quickly.'

Jenny stayed in her room and closed her door until it was open only a crack. She wasn't sure why, but she hid behind the crack in her door and watched as Helen ushered a man who looked about sixty-five down the hall and into the kitchen.

Jo? Where had Jenny heard that name? Helen had talked about a 'Dr Jo' in her strange phone conversation. Jenny wanted to know what was going on, so as quietly as she could, she pushed open her door and walked along the corridor. There was a chair beside the telephone table in the hall, and Jenny sat in it. The door to the kitchen was slightly open, and Jenny could just see in.

The man was dressed in a suit and carried a briefcase, which he opened on the kitchen table to reveal a stethoscope and other doctorish-looking things. Jenny shifted her position a little on the chair so that she could see better.

'We started his new treatment,' Helen said.

'I see,' said Dr Jo, 'and he's been experiencing lethargy?'

'Yes, yesterday he was very sleepy. He's seems okay today, but I thought we should have you check him over anyway.'

'Of course. I'll check you over as well while I'm here. And ask John to come and see me some time soon. You need to keep up regular medical examinations, you know.'

'Thank you, Jo, I don't know what we'd do without you.'

'Well, I'm not getting any younger, you know. You'll not be able to rely on me for ever.'

Helen's voice got quieter. She said something that Jenny couldn't hear. Dr Jo shook his head. Helen spoke again, her face looked almost pleading.

'No,' said Dr Jo, 'you know how I feel about that. I'm happy to look after your medical needs while I can, but I want nothing more to do with it.'

Helen nodded, accepting his decision.

'I'll get Stephen then,' she said, moving towards the door.

Jenny stood up quickly and backed away closer to her room. When Helen came through the door Jenny rubbed her eyes and said, 'Hi, I just woke up. I'm going to watch TV, if that's all right?'

Helen smiled at her, showing no signs that she was aware of Jenny's eavesdropping. 'Sure.' She followed Jenny into the living room and turned on the TV, then left, closing the door behind her.

Jenny ignored the home make-over programme that was on TV, and thought about what she'd seen and heard. What was Stephen's new treatment that they'd started? What had Helen asked the doctor that made him shake his head? What had made him say he wanted nothing more to do with it? She wished she'd been able to hear more of their conversation.

A little while later she turned off the TV and opened the door to leave the living room. The doctor was being shown out, and he glanced in her direction. She smiled at him, and the smile he returned her was abrupt, almost nervous, and then he turned quickly away.

Seven

The days until Jenny's next hospital appointment went quickly. When Stephen was there she played with him, when he was at day care she worked with Helen in the garage workshop. Her pottery skills were slowly improving, as was her ocarina playing. She read Mandy's diaries when she could snatch a moment in the daytime. She didn't seem to be able to stay awake to read them when she went to bed at night. Whether she sat with Helen and John in the living room watching TV and drinking the ritual night-time cocoa, or whether Helen brought her some in her room, she always fell asleep without even thinking about it. She began to crave her cocoa in the evenings, making excuses to go to bed early so Helen would bring it to her sooner. She had worried about sleeping in a room on her own, without Hayley's banter to protect her from her night-time fears, but now it seemed that all she needed was cocoa.

Her balance was improving too. She could now take steps without having to screw up her face in concentration, and she even occasionally bobbed and swayed to music from the radio that often played in Helen's kitchen. She began to wonder about going out on her own. Could she catch a bus? Could she walk around the shops? These two things were both her dreams and her nightmares. To have freedom, to have experiences like other fourteen-year-olds, to look at make-up and magazines, of course she wanted that. But getting a bus? She remembered riding buses with her friends before the accident. The big step up, the jolting motion of the bus stopping and starting – even with two legs it had been difficult to stay on her feet. And walking around the shops ... doors would be a problem, but then lots of shops had automatic doors now, didn't they? But what if the shops were crowded with people, what if people bumped and jostled her? Would she fall? Would she be able to get up?

Still, the idea niggled at her, became almost an obsession.

It was on her mind as she rode in the ambulance towards the hospital.

Her voice was hoarse as she answered the friendly questions of the ambulance crew. She'd woken up with a bit of a sore throat, and also a strange feeling in her chest that she thought must be heartburn.

She hadn't brought her chair at all, just her legs and crutches. When they pulled up outside the hospital entrance, Jenny asked the ambulance crew just to leave her outside the door. She said she would be fine from there.

'Aren't we getting very independent?' said Jim the

driver, a big black man who made Jenny laugh frequently with his humorous banter.

'Well, I don't know about you, Jim, but I am,' Jenny shot back, smiling.

The ambulance didn't drive off after she climbed out, but waited to see her safely through the front door. She was both irritated and comforted by its presence. Wearing her legs, she drew fewer stares than when she was in her chair. Especially when, like today, she wore long trousers that covered up the prosthetics. She had crutches, but then so did lots of people going into the hospital. She walked up the ramp. Her gait was smoother and less obviously disabled than it had been since the accident, and as she mingled with the crowds of people going into the hospital she felt almost normal. At the door she turned and blew a cheeky kiss at Jim in the ambulance, her confidence at walking spilling over and making her bold. He tooted his horn and drove away.

Walking to the lift, she passed a group of teenage boys who made some comments that she couldn't hear. She sneaked a look at them and saw them giving her appreciative glances. While she knew that, if she showed them her legs, that would be the end of their appreciation, she still enjoyed the attention, and giggled slightly as she got into the lift. She guessed she was kind of good-looking. Not her legs, of course, but the rest of her body was slim and shapely, and her face was pretty enough. She'd washed her hair that morning; it was shoulder-length and straight and nut-brown. She usually wore it tied back, but had left it down that morning, looking shiny and blow-dried. Why shouldn't boys fancy her?

She had to go to a different floor than usual, to see about her new prosthetics. She spoke to Dr Evans's receptionist, who showed her to a seating area where she could wait to be called.

She sat down, leaning her crutches against the wall beside her, and took out the latest of Mandy's diaries that she was reading.

Mandy had turned twelve, and her dad had given her a little jewellery box as a birthday present. Her parents were still fighting, and sometimes the fights had turned violent. Jenny wondered when social services were going to get involved, as she was sure they must be if Mandy was going to be taken into care. She shuddered as she read Mandy's accounts of the shouting and screaming of her parents. She felt more than ever that she was intruding on Mandy's private world. And yet she felt compelled to read on. Like picking a scab that hurts but can't be left alone, she read the black, poisoned words that Mandy's parents said to each other. She read the angry, hurt words that Mandy confided to her diary. How she was afraid, how she felt lost, unloved, forgotten. She held her breath as Mandy described her mother throwing a glass bowl full of trifle at her father. She gasped when she read what he called her, when she read that he hit her.

When the nurse came to call Jenny in for her appointment, she jumped as if she had been hit herself, and then laughed with the bemused nurse, telling her she'd been miles away.

Casts had to be made of her stumps so that the new prosthetics would be exact fits. Dr Evans showed her some legs that would be similar to her new ones. They were attached by suction to her stumps, an improvement on the straps she was used to. She had to start wearing tight socks that would fit under the cups of the prosthetic legs when they were made. Dr Evans explained how it would take a while for her to adjust to her new legs, but that other people wearing suction cups found them comfortable, and once she got used to them she would find them an improvement over the old ones. They were more modern and expensive, and she was only getting them because of his funding grant.

Dr Evans was in a good mood, and as he took the measurements of her stumps, he chatted away to her, telling her about his trip to America and how excited he was about the whole skiing trip project. Jenny couldn't help but feel buoyed up by his enthusiasm, both about the trip and her new legs, so much so that she barely noticed the guilt that was always there shadowing her feelings about skiing.

She was a little late for physio, but they knew about her earlier appointment, so that didn't matter. The boy with one foot missing was there already. He had got his new prosthetic foot and Jenny joined in admiring it. He introduced himself to her as Craig, and told her he was twelve. They chatted a bit, and Jenny thought how silly she had been to avoid talking to him before. It felt better to have a friend and what did it matter what anyone else thought?

She told the physio working with her about the incident with the kitchen knife when she'd been making sandwiches, and they did some work on how Jenny could regain her balance if something knocked into her like that. It wasn't easy: it required a lot of strength in her stumps, holding them steady even if her legs were at odd angles. It also took courage, to cope with something unexpected; the sort of thing that toddlers learn by falling over a lot and getting up again. But being fourteen is not like being a toddler. There's further to fall to start with, and more embarrassment and fear, and it's harder to learn anything new. The session was difficult and by the end of it Jenny's mood was not as buoyant as it had been, and she could feel several bruises forming in spite of the mats that had broken her many falls.

When she got back to the Hollands' house, Helen was doing some home-schooling work with Stephen, so Jenny gratefully excused herself and went and lay on her bed with Mandy's diary.

Tuesday 14th January

> Mum and Dad have gone out, thank goodness. They've probably gone to buy more glass things to throw at each other. Not that we have any money to buy anything with. If I ask Mum for anything I get the same answer: NO. 'Sorry, love,

we've got no money.' 'Sorry, love, we can't afford it.' Dad seems to find money to buy beer though.

Yesterday I left my new jewellery box on the floor in the bathroom. Only 'cos I wanted to look at it better and there's more light in there. But Dad went mental. I think he must have stood on it when he went to the toilet in the morning. Okay, so I shouldn't have left it on the floor, but I just forgot. Not exactly a crime, is it? But he started shouting about how I didn't deserve any presents and why did he waste his bloody money on me? And he said he was going to take it back to the shop and get his money back. And I cried and said I was sorry, and I didn't want him to take it 'cos I really like it, and then he said okay, he wouldn't take it back, but I could see that he was looking at it thinking he could get more money for beer if he did, so I quickly took it to my room. I've got this really great idea, anyway. I saw it on *Blue Peter*, about burying things and digging them up years later, to remember how things were like. So I'm going to bury my jewellery box, even though I love it, but at least it would stop him from stealing it. I could dig it up after ten years and by then I'll be old enough to live on my own. I told Alison about my idea, and she's gonna come round and help, and we're going to go to the park on Princes Street, 'cos there's bushes and things behind where the swings are and we could bury it *there, and no one would find it there, and we'll both put our photographs in and write a letter about what we are like so that when we dig it up it will be a real laugh.*

The park on Princes Street? I know that park, Jenny thought. It was near where she used to live, and when she was a little girl her mum had taken her there and pushed her on the swings. Could she once have seen Mandy there? She tried to remember if she'd ever seen any Orphan Annie lookalikes burying things in the bushes. She was forgetting that she didn't actually know what Mandy looked like, that she'd made up the Orphan Annie thing. As she thought, an idea started to take root in her mind: she would go to the park. She'd get the bus. She'd dig up Mandy's box. There was a line drawing in the diary showing where the box was hidden – like a treasure map. She'd bury it again, of course, so if Mandy came back for it, it would still be there. Maybe she'd add a note of her own, about having found the diaries, and she'd put in her phone number so Mandy could contact her. Jenny felt her excitement rising thinking about it.

But what would she tell Helen? I just have to go out for an hour or two – oh and I'll need money for bus fare and a spade. Yeah, right, that wouldn't arouse any suspicion. And digging? Yes, she was getting better at walking, but was she really up to digging for treasure?

Her thoughts were interrupted by the phone ringing, and a few moments later by Helen calling her name.

She got up and went through to the hall where Helen was talking into the phone.

'I'm really glad to hear that, Lee. I knew you'd find a good home, you're a great person.'

Lee! Jenny's insides leapt. So he had taken the hint when she'd put her phone number on the note she sent him. She took the phone from Helen with a smile, and went back into her room.

'Lee, how are you?' she asked, after she'd lain back down on the bed.

'I'm good,' he said. 'I have a brother now.'

'Really? A brother? Me too. What's he like?'

'Oh, you know, a bit of a pain. Ouch!'

Evidently the brother was there with Lee.

'So, um, I wondered, um . . .' Now Lee started to sound embarrassed, and Jenny wondered what was coming next.

'What? Spit it out!'

'Oh, you're sensitive as ever, I see,' Lee laughed.

'I'm sorry, but go on, tell me. What did you wonder?'

Lee spoke without pausing for breath between words, as if he was afraid he would lose his nerve if he slowed down. 'IwonderedifyouwantedtocomeoutwithmetoMcDonaldsorsomething?'

It took a second for Jenny to decipher the individual words. 'Did you just ask me out on a date?'

'Yeah.'

'Actually,' said Jenny, realising that as well as a dream-come-true moment, this was the perfect solution to the problem of digging up Mandy's box, 'I would love to go out with you. How about we go to the park on Princes Street? Oh, and could you bring a spade and money for the bus fare?'

'What? Jenny, have you gone even more mental?'

'No! Listen, I'll explain it all when you come. Oh, and make it a small spade, like a trowel or something, so that you can hide it in your bag. And . . .'

'And what? Make sure I wear a false moustache and say the secret password?'

'No! I was going to say thank you. And I can't wait to see you again.'

'Oh. Well, you're welcome, and I'm kind of looking forward to seeing you too.'

They talked for a while longer, and arranged for Lee to come round the next day. His foster parents said they would drop him off, and then they could get the bus together. Jenny asked Helen if it would be all right and Helen seemed a bit surprised, but said yes. After Jenny had hung up the phone she did a little whoop (that hurt her sore throat, but she didn't care) and fell back on her bed grinning at the ceiling.

'Lee asked me out.'

'*Lee* asked me out.'

'Lee asked *me* out.'

'Lee asked me *out*.'

She felt a slight throbbing on her chin and touched it with her hand. 'Typical,' she said out loud, although her grin only faltered slightly. 'My first date and I've got a zit.'

The zit was worse in the morning, but with a little bit of make-up it didn't look too bad. Jenny spent longer than usual getting dressed and washing her hair. She wore some eyeliner and lipstick and she was pleased with the effect.

'Look at you!' said Helen, when she finally made it down to breakfast. 'Lee's a lucky boy.'

Jenny blushed, but smiled as she sat down to tea and toast. She was just brushing the last of the crumbs from her fingers when the doorbell rang. Helen answered the door and Jenny could faintly hear her talking to Lee. She got up from her seat, a thing that she still did quite awkwardly, and was standing up when Lee entered the kitchen.

'Whoa,' he said, 'you look great.'

Stephen ran in from the living room, pushing past Jenny in his eagerness to get to Lee. Jenny wobbled, and if it hadn't been for her extra balance training at physio she would probably have fallen.

'Oh Jenny, let me help you,' said Lee, rushing towards her.

'No, it's okay,' said Jenny. 'I'm fine.' She'd kept her balance and smiled as if nothing had happened.

She watched Lee with Stephen, and could instantly see how fond they were of each other. When she felt she'd shared Lee enough, she caught his eye again and said, 'Let me show you my pots.'

Jenny led Lee to the workshop, leaving Helen and Stephen behind in the kitchen. He admired her handi-work dutifully, and listened to her play a tune on her ocarina.

'You're good at that,' he said. 'I could never get the

hang of it. I blew too hard or too soft, or something like that.'

Jenny laughed at him and turned to leave the work-shop.

'My goodness,' said Lee.

Jenny turned around. 'What?'

'The door to the forbidden room is open.'

'What are you talking about? That door? It just goes down to the cellar where the kiln is. Stephen's not allowed down there because of the heat, and I don't do stairs anyway.'

'It was always locked when I lived here, but the floor beside it was clean, in an arc, as if the door was regularly opened. I always thought there must be something hidden down there. It was like a big mystery to me. I even thought about trying to break in, you know, like they do in the films, picking the lock with a hairpin or something. But then they sent me back to Oak Hall, so I never did.'

Jenny looked at him searchingly. She wasn't going to say anything to him about her suspicions, but if he had felt that there were mysteries at the Hollands' house too, maybe she should.

'I could go down and look,' said Lee. 'Now, while there's only you and me here.'

Jenny stared at him, suddenly scared and excited. She nodded.

There was a moment of indecision, when they both stood looking at the open door, but just as Lee took a step towards it, the door from the kitchen opened and Helen leaned her head into the workshop.

'There's a bus due in ten minutes that stops near the crossroads. You should get going if you want to catch it.'

Jenny stared at Helen, and then realised that if her face was anything like Lee's, then they both had very guilty expressions. She forced herself to smile.

'Oh yeah. Let's get going, Lee.'

'Where are you off to anyway?' Helen asked, as they left the workshop.

'Oh, just to the park.'

'I could drive you.'

'No, it's okay,' Jenny said. 'I want to try getting a bus, to see if I can cope.'

'I might take her out to lunch too, if that's okay with you,' Lee added. 'McDonald's.'

Jenny hadn't been to McDonald's in years, and her mouth watered at the prospect, even though she'd just had breakfast.

'Okay,' said Helen. 'Have fun.'

Jenny deliberated about whether to bring her crutches. Without them she walked much more slowly, and she would get tired sooner, but with them she wouldn't be able to hold hands with Lee. In the end she did bring them, her head winning over her heart, although once they got out of view of the house, Lee took one of the crutches off her and held her hand anyway.

They didn't quite make it to the bus stop in time for the bus, but thankfully, when Lee waved her crutch in the air, the bus stopped for them anyway. Jenny worried about stepping on to it. She wasn't sure if she really wanted Lee to lift her, but feared that it might come to that. As it happened, the bus driver noticed her difficulty.

'Hang on a minute, love,' he said, and did something that made the side of the bus lower slowly until Jenny could step on with just a little bit of help from Lee. One or two people on the bus looked to see what the hold-up was, but when they noticed Jenny's crutches they quickly looked away again.

The bus driver waited until they were seated before he started off again, and Jenny felt greatly relieved that two of her fears at least had not been realised.

Sitting on the bus with Lee felt so wonderful that Jenny almost wanted to cry. Get a grip on yourself, girl, she said silently, taking deep breaths to calm herself.

The day was warm, but Jenny noticed dark clouds forming in one corner of the sky. Lee saw her looking at them and said, 'Don't worry – if it rains we can always dig ourselves a shelter.' He showed her the small metal trowel in his bag.

Jenny smiled. 'I suppose you want me to explain why I asked you to bring that?'

'Well, I was kind of wondering.'

Jenny started telling Lee about finding Mandy's diary and reading it. Thankfully, he seemed more interested than Hayley had when Jenny had tried to tell her.

'Wow,' said Lee, 'that's pretty cool. I wonder when she lived there. I thought I was the first one they'd fostered. You should read ahead.'

Jenny had wondered about skipping through to the

most recent diary, but something stopped her. It was as if she was reading a novel, and to read the end first would spoil it. She didn't want to argue with Lee, though. 'Maybe,' she said.

The bus stopped right outside the park. Lee took her hand to help her off. He held her crutch in his other hand and leaned on it as if he needed it. She could only imagine what they must have looked like, with a crutch on each side and holding hands in the middle. Still, once again she found she didn't care what she looked like to other people, or what they thought of her.

There weren't many people in the park anyway. Perhaps the ominous clouds had put them off. They walked past the ducks and swans in the pond, who followed them hopefully for a while. Then they walked to the playground.

Seeing the playground brought stabs of memory back to Jenny. Being here with Eve, running, laughing, climbing. She tried to fight the memories back, to stop them from intruding on her time with Lee. He was talking to her, but she barely heard a word he said.

'Jenny . . . Jenny . . . hello?'

'Hmm, what?'

'I said, do you know which bush we should dig up, 'cos there's lots of them.'

'Um, yeah, well . . . look at this.'

She led him to a bench and they sat down. She took one of Mandy's diaries from her bag and opened it where she'd folded over the corner of a page, and showed Lee the picture of the park. The swings, the climbing frame, the roundabout, the paths to the pond and the toilets were drawn and labelled. Jenny tried to align it with what they could see in front of them. She could see the paths and the swings as they were in the drawing, but the roundabout and the climbing frame seemed to be in different positions, and the little animal-shaped seats that bounced about on top of big metal springs weren't on the page at all.

'Either she's a really bad drawer,' said Lee, 'or the park's changed since she was here.'

Jenny looked at the climbing frame and the other play equipment in the park. They looked fairly modern, but not that new. Some of the things had changed since she'd been there with Eve, but the climbing frame had been there then, and for as long as she could remember. How old were Mandy's diaries?

'Well, it looks like the bushes are still in the same places anyway,' Jenny said. 'So if that's the swings, and that's the path to the pond, then the climbing frame must be where the roundabout used to be, and the box must be buried … there.' Jenny pointed first at the diagram, and then at an actual bush, a large gnarled woody thing with evil-looking prickly thorns. 'Between that bush and the wall.'

'Great,' said Lee. 'I guess I'll be the one digging then.'

Jenny smiled sweetly at him. 'Thank you,' she said.

'It's just as well for you that I like you so much, isn't it?'

Jenny's pulse quickened, and she wasn't sure if it was because of Lee's words or the prospect of seeing Mandy's box. She watched him from the bench, as he pushed his way past the bush and stooped down behind it.

'Ouch!' he said. 'It's trying to eat me.'

Jenny ignored his comment. 'Can you see anything?'

'There's about twenty years' worth of leaves and acorns and things. It's not so much digging as just brushing all that aside.'

'Oh.' Jenny watched for the glimpses she got of Lee between the leafy branches of the bushes, and heard him grunt and occasionally cry out in pain as a thorn scratched him. She wondered for the first time if it was fair expecting Lee to do this for her. Not a great first date, really.

'Are you digging yet?' she asked him.

'Yeah.' Lee was panting with the effort.

Jenny decided to have a look. She struggled to her feet and walked over.

'Let me see,' she said.

Lee straightened up and helped pull her past the prickly branches until they were huddled together in the space between the bush and the old brick wall. Jenny looked into the hole that Lee was digging. It was quite deep, with no sign of Mandy's box.

'Maybe you should stop,' she said.

'Arr,' said Lee, in a funny mock-pirate's voice, 'but, cap'n, I be wantin' my share of the doubloons.'

'The whats?'

'Doubloons. That's pirate gold. Don't you know anything?'

'Oh. Okay.'

Just then it started to rain. Not gentle light drizzle either, but heavy lashing rain that felt like someone was throwing buckets of water at them. The wall gave them some shelter at least, and they leaned against it, looking into the hole, which was filling up with water that soaked into the earth, only to be filled up again as the rain persisted.

'Oh, look!' said Jenny suddenly. 'The rain is washing away the soil . . . there's something underneath . . . something shiny! Look!'

Eight

The rain was indeed washing the soil off something flat and shiny. Lee crouched down and used his fingers to dig further round the edges of whatever it was. Jenny, feeling excited and impatient, longed to get down beside him, but she hadn't covered crouching in physio yet and had to content herself with leaning against the wall and watching. At least she was staying relatively dry; poor Lee was completely drenched, his straight dark hair looking as if it was painted in streaks across his head, and large droplets of water clinging to the ends of his eyelashes.

'Is it the box?' Jenny found she had to shout over the sound of the pounding rain.

'I don't know. I think so. Hang on.'

Lee slid his hand into the hole, and the soil around the box shook and rose as his fingers curled underneath it. He began to pull.

'It's coming, I think.'

For what seemed like a long time Lee battled with the box, but finally he rose, shaking wet earth off what appeared to be a very rusty old biscuit tin. They looked at the tin and they looked at each other, their faces like children on Christmas morning.

As suddenly as the rain had started, it stopped, and the sun was out again within moments. Lee shook his head like a dog, and water sprayed off him, leaving his hair looking spiky. 'Oh thanks,' said Jenny, whose face had taken the brunt of Lee's shaking.

'You're welcome,' he said, and leaned forward and kissed her.

The kiss started as a friendly peck. A 'we did it' kind of kiss. And then there was a moment, a split second in time, when the kiss might have ended, and they might have stayed 'just good friends'. A moment that lasted hours and barely a second. Lee's lips brushed Jenny's. He stopped. She hardly dared to breathe. She looked at his eyes, one of the raindrops still clinging to his lashes. She saw her own face reflected in his pupils. She was smiling. And then they kissed again, and this time it was no friendly peck.

The kiss was thrilling and wonderful. Longed for and yet unexpected. When they stopped, Jenny's smile returned unbidden.

'I'd be weak at the knees right now if I had any,' she joked.

But Lee didn't laugh; he was staring at her as if he was trying to take in every tiny detail of her.

'I love you, Jenny.'

Jenny's smile faltered and her lip began to quiver. Her eyes felt hot and wet.

'What? What is it, Jenny? Don't cry. I'm sorry.'

'I'm not crying.' Her voice cracked and wavered. 'Well, maybe I am. But don't be sorry. I'm not sorry. I just can't believe it. I thought you'd never . . . Well . . . because . . . I . . . I love you too.'

And now Lee did smile. A big grin that lit up his face.

He was still holding the box. As Jenny's eyes lowered shyly, she saw it and for a moment couldn't remember what it was. Then reality came back to her and she said, 'Oh! Mandy's box.'

Lee looked down at his hands as if he too had forgotten what he was holding. He raised his eyebrows in an expression that Jenny found completely adorable.

'Let's open it.'

'Yes!'

Lee went over to the bench and put the box down, then came back to help Jenny. Out of the shade of the shrubbery he looked grubby, his face and hands streaked with mud. Jenny laughed. 'Look at you, you're all dirty.'

'You're not so clean yourself,' he said, laughing. Their smiles fell, though, as they sat on the bench and looked at the box.

The moment felt reverent. Jenny gently, tentatively put her hands on the lid and tried to lift it.

It wouldn't budge.

Feeling a little silly for expecting a gentle pull to work, she lifted the box and rested it on her lap, ignoring the rusty and muddy smears it left on her trousers. She lifted one end and tried to prise open the corner. She thought she felt some movement, but not enough to get the lid off.

'Let me try,' Lee said.

She handed the box over, and Lee tried a similar technique to hers. Nothing happened and Jenny was just about to suggest they bring it home and try a knife or something, when the lid suddenly came off in Lee's hands and the box's contents flew out.

A glittery cube about ten centimetres square remained in the tin, but yellowing papers danced in the wind as they fell to the ground. Lee bent down and scooped them up, shaking drops of puddle water off them.

Jenny took the cube, which must have been Mandy's jewellery box, and looked at it. It was made of clear plastic, not even glass, with coloured stones set around the edges. It was pretty, but obviously not worth very much money. Jenny suddenly felt pangs of sympathy for Mandy, who had been so pleased with this little trinket. Lee had sorted out two letters and one square photograph.

They looked at the photo first. It was black and white. Within the white edges that framed the picture, two girls stood smiling. Neither looked like Orphan Annie, but nevertheless Jenny assumed they were Mandy and Alison. The picture was difficult to make out: the girl's faces were small and the print was grainy. The clothes they wore were strange, with floral prints and big collars, but they looked happy, as if they'd just shared a joke.

'Whoa, black and white,' said Lee. 'How long ago did people use black and white film?'

'You still can,' said Jenny, although her voice sounded puzzled, 'for arty portraits and things.'

'Suppose,' said Lee. 'But that doesn't look like much of an arty portrait. More like something someone's longsighted granny would take.'

'Yeah.'

They looked at the letters next, reading the one signed 'Amanda Jean Patterson' first.

'Whoa,' said Jenny, when she'd finished.

The most surprising thing about the letter was the date.

Amanda Jean Patterson, with her best friend, Alison Cooper, buried this box on Tuesday 21st January 1975. To be dug up by Alison and me on or around 21st January 1985, when I will be an old lady of 22.

Hello old me.

I will write some things about me to jog your memory in case you've forgotten. My favourite colour is purple. My favourite fab pop star is the gorgeous Donny Osmond. My favourite TV programmes are Blue Peter and Are you being Served (I'm free!).

The jewellery box is my treasured possession, even though it was given to me by Dad, who I hate.

I hope that when you read this you are happy and not living with Mum and Dad anymore.

Forever yours
Amanda Jean Patterson

The other note was written by Alison, and was much the same as Mandy's.

When they'd read both the letters, Lee and Jenny looked at each other.

'1975! That's over thirty years ago,' Lee said. 'She must have lived in the house before the Hollands.'

'She'd be in her forties now,' Jenny said, with shock in her voice. 'I wonder why she never dug up her box.'

They sat in silence for a moment, contemplating their discovery.

Jenny swallowed, and noticed that her throat was still a little bit sore. She coughed dryly, and the coughing made her eyes water.

'You all right?' said Lee. 'Are you choking?'

'No, I'm fine. I just woke up with a bit of a sore throat yesterday. It hurts when I swallow, and it feels scratchy. It's weird because I feel a bit burny in my chest as well – not when I breathe, but when I eat. I think maybe it's heartburn, but I've never had that before, so I'm not really sure. It's much better today than yesterday anyway.'

'Really,' said Lee, sounding genuinely interested. 'I used to get that. I'd wake up with a sore throat and a burning feeling in my chest, and it'd be gone in a day or two. Hasn't happened in ages, though – not since I was at the Hollands' actually. Funny that.'

Jenny was suddenly interested. 'This happened to you at the Hollands' and not anywhere else?'

'Well, yeah, I suppose. Maybe it's all the cocoa they give you.'

'Maybe.'

'What's with all that cocoa anyway? It's like they have shares in Cadbury's or something.'

Jenny laughed. 'Yeah. Just their habit, I suppose.'

She wondered about telling Lee about the biohazard box and the overheard phone call about 'running tests'. And the other things that had seemed strange to her, like the surgical gloves in the kitchen waste bin and the doctor who 'wanted no part' in something. As she thought about it, though, it sounded kind of lame. Nothing to tell really.

'I'm hungry,' said Lee, cutting through her thoughts. 'How about we bury that box and go to McDonalds?'

Jenny had fully intended to bury the box again. She'd brought a letter to put in it, about her finding the diaries. But that was when she thought Mandy was nearer their age. When she thought the box was buried only a few years ago. Now she didn't know what to do. She took the note out of her bag. It was sealed in an envelope with 'Mandy' written on the front. She'd written about finding the diaries, and told Mandy to call her when she dug up the box. She'd given the number of Oak Hall, figuring they would be able to trace her even if she'd moved on. She didn't think she'd dated the letter. Scrambling in her bag for a pen, she decided to write the date on the envelope and put the letter in the box. Mandy might come back one day, and even if she was a grown woman, she might want her diaries back.

Lee put the box back in the hole and scraped the soil

and leaves back over it. Thinking that Mandy might not be able to find it, not having her own map that she'd drawn in her diary, he made an M with sticks and laid it over the spot where the box was buried.

'M marks the spot,' he said aloud.

They went to the public toilets in the park to get washed. Luckily there was a disabled toilet so Jenny could sit down and reach the sink. Their clothes were still muddy, but at least their faces and hands were clean as they set off for the high street.

Jenny stared at Lee over her Big Mac and fries. She couldn't quite believe that they'd kissed. She'd never had a boyfriend before, never kissed a boy before. And Lee ... well, he was almost like a brother in some ways, because they'd lived at the home together – although she'd never thought of him as a brother. She'd felt differently about Lee since they'd both arrived at Oak Hall.

She remembered the day they met. Both escorted by social workers, her from the hospital, Lee from wherever he lived before Oak Hall. They'd waited outside Sarah's office. The oak-panelled walls and red-patterned carpet in the lobby that now seemed so commonplace to Jenny had then seemed austere and a little frightening. The two social workers had smiled, exchanged pleasantries. She had tried to look at Lee without being obvious. She'd caught him looking at her, and they'd both blushed and turned away. Even then she'd found him intriguing. Before the accident she'd started to notice boys of course, but not really since. Something about Lee had drawn her, though.

Sarah had spoken to them both separately, and then brought them together to be introduced to the other children. That gave them some kind of bond. They were the new ones. Even though new children arrived frequently at Oak Hall, still Lee and Jenny felt linked by arriving together. Hayley had taken Jenny under her wing then, and Lee had gone off with some of the boys, but still they sought each other out. They were soulmates. If either of them had problems they wanted to talk about, it was the other one they turned to. Jenny had always felt electricity when she was with him, but she'd hidden it, never thinking her feelings could be reciprocated. She assumed any boy would be repulsed by her legs. She assumed Lee was.

But now he'd kissed her. Could it be that he could fancy a girl with no legs?

Lee was eating chicken nuggets, dunking them in ketchup then throwing them whole into his mouth. He had ketchup smeared around one corner of his mouth and even that endeared him to Jenny.

She would happily just have gazed at him, but she felt she should be saying something. Even though she'd decided not to, she blurted out, 'There's something weird about the Hollands, though, don't you think?'

Lee spoke around the food in his mouth.

'Weird how?'

'Oh, I don't know. It's nothing really, just . . . well, little things.'

'Like what?'

'Um, well,' Jenny blushed, 'this is going to sound crazy, but I'm sure I heard Helen saying on the phone to John that she was "running tests" on me. And John brought home a box from work that said 'Biohazards' on it, and he said it was paperwork, but I heard glass bottles inside it.'

'Weird,' Lee agreed. 'Did she actually say she was running tests on Jenny?'

'Well, no, but . . .'

'And John could have been doing paperwork about something in a bottle.'

'Yeah. You're right. I'm being stupid.'

'But,' said Lee, 'on the other hand . . . there is the secret underground room. And Stephen is exceptionally smart for a five-year-old. Maybe they're planning to suck out your brain and feed it to their son in their underground lab.' He finished off his sentence with a peal of evil laughter. 'Mwahahaha!'

Jenny laughed. 'Maybe that's what they did to you, and that's why you're so dumb!'

'Aw,' said Lee, looking hurt.

'I didn't mean it,' Jenny said. 'Dummy.'

He threw a chip at her and she threw one back. They caught the disapproving look of a mother whose children had started to copy their chip-throwing.

They stopped and primly sat up straight, like model teenagers, while stifling their giggles.

'I've had enough anyway,' Jenny said, looking at the remains of her burger. 'They're not as good as I remembered.'

128

'I'll have yours then,' said Lee, swooping on the rest of Jenny's burger and finishing it off in two bites.

Lee handed Jenny her crutches and helped her out of her seat. The mother watched him and looked guilty, as if she wouldn't have disapproved of their food fight if she'd known Jenny was disabled. They didn't give her another thought, though, as they left the restaurant.

'You should ring me,' Lee said, out of the blue.

'Hmm?'

'If you think something funny is going on at the Hollands'. Or if you see anything else that makes you suspicious. I'll give you my mobile number.'

'Since when have you had a mobile?'

'Since my foster parents gave me one. They said it would be handy if I needed them to pick me up or something.'

'Cool. Do you think I should ask John and Helen for one?'

Lee considered. 'Hmm. Probably not. You could drop hints, though.'

'They probably don't think there's any point in getting me a mobile,' Jenny said. 'They don't think I'm independent enough.' There was some bitterness in Jenny's voice. Not so much directed at the Hollands – who, to be fair, had not really treated her disability as such a big deal – as at the world in general and her own frustrations in particular.

'But look at you today,' Lee said. 'Getting the bus, going to McDonald's, digging up some old lady's jewellery box.'

'Yeah,' Jenny laughed. 'Couldn't have done it without you, though.'

'Of course you could, Jenny,' Lee said, flashing her a smile. 'You can do anything you want. You're brilliant.'

'Yeah,' said Jenny, almost believing it. 'I am, aren't I?'

Lee got the bus back with Jenny and they walked together down the lane through the trees. Lee said they should ask the Hollands if they could camp out in the woods some time.

'Yeah, right,' said Jenny. 'Like they'd let us! Besides, it's probably private land or something – we'd be trespassing.'

'Hmm', said Lee. 'Maybe. But I never saw anyone anywhere near the house or the woods except the Hollands. Have you?'

Jenny hadn't, except for the ambulance coming to take her to physio. 'I still don't think they'd let us, though,' she said.

When they got to the house, Helen and Stephen were in the front garden collecting leaves.

'We're going to make a picture out of leaves and twigs and things and Mummy's going to put it on the wall.' Stephen told them. 'Will you help us, Jenny? You have to find big leaves and little leaves and interesting leaves. I've got some oak leaves, look.'

John came out and offered to take Lee home, and Jenny agreed to stay outside with Stephen and Helen, although she just sat on a bench and watched as she was already exhausted.

John had been gone about ten minutes when they

heard the sound of a car in the lane. Helen stood bolt upright and listened. Jenny thought she looked like an animal looking for predators, like a programme she saw once about meerkats, standing on their back legs when they heard a threatening sound.

'It's too soon for John to be back,' she said, as if she was talking to herself, and then she said more loudly, 'Stephen, let's go inside now. You too, Jenny. Come on, let me help you.'

She grabbed Jenny's arm and rushed her and Stephen around to the side of the house and in through the back door. They'd barely got inside when they heard the crunching of a car pulling up on the gravel outside the front door, and then footsteps followed by the ringing of the bell.

Helen stayed completely still, and raised her finger to her lips. 'Let's pretend we're not in,' she whispered, with a smile that looked not quite real. 'I'm not expecting anyone; it's probably just someone trying to sell something.'

The doorbell rang again, and Stephen giggled softly.

'We don't want to buy anything,' he told Jenny conspiratorially.

After a minute or two they heard footsteps again, and then the sound of a car door and someone driving off. Helen let out a breath she must have been holding in, then smiled as if nothing had happened and said she would get them drinks and after that they would make their picture.

Stephen jumped up and down with excitement and Jenny excused herself and went to her room.

Inside her room she thought about what had just happened. Helen had been hiding from someone. But she didn't even know who it was. Was Helen just really shy? Or did she not want whoever it was to see me? Or Stephen? Jenny remembered how Helen had told her that they didn't get post delivered because they didn't want the postman calling at the house all the time.

Suddenly Jenny felt scared. Too many small, strange things were adding up to something big. The Hollands lived in a house in the middle of nowhere and they hid if anyone came to call. She heard Helen talking about 'running tests' and she found surgical gloves in the bin. John brought home something from his job in the lab and lied about what it was. The doctor said he wanted nothing to do with something. But what? What was going on? Was there some terrible secret at the Hollands', or was she just getting carried away over nothing?

Nine

The next few weeks went by quickly for Jenny and nothing else strange happened, so she dismissed her suspicions as silliness. She saw Lee about once a week. They went to the cinema, something Jenny hadn't done since before the accident and which made her very excited. She went to Lee's house and met his foster parents. His foster mum, a tiny Chinese woman called May, cooked loads of delicious food, while his foster dad, an enormous man built like a rugby player, larked about with Lee and his foster brother David. May called Lee 'Chan', and Jenny asked him about it when they were alone.

'Chan is my first name,' Lee said.

'What? I thought Lee was your first name.'

Lee laughed. 'Everybody thinks that. Chinese people put their surname first and their given name second. So many people got it mixed up, though, that I just decided to let everyone call me Lee.'

Jenny screwed up her face. 'Lee is your last name?'

'Yeah.'

'Would you prefer me to call you Chan?'

'You can call me Lee, or Chan, or sweetheart, or

handsome hunk, whatever you like.'

Jenny looked at Lee, and tried to make her mind think 'Chan'. But she was so used to thinking of him as Lee that her mind balked at the change.

'I could call you Ackerman,' said Lee, 'if it makes you feel any better. Or Moonchild, or Firstjoy.'

'AHH!' Jenny shrieked. 'How do you know about my names?'

Lee looked sheepish.

'On the day we arrived at Oak Hall Sarah had both our files on her desk and I kind of read yours.'

'But you never said till now.'

'Yeah, I guessed you didn't want people to know those names, because you never told anyone. And . . .'

He smiled and looked a little embarrassed.

'And what?'

'Well, I liked knowing a secret about you. It made me feel closer to you.'

Jenny found it difficult to be annoyed after a comment like that, but still she said, 'You must swear never to tell anyone.'

Lee looked contrite. 'Okay, I swear,' he said, 'although I don't know why you're so embarrassed. I think they're cool names.'

Jenny rolled her eyes and said, '*Pleeeease*!'

'They'll be our secret,' said Lee, 'Moonchild.'

One day they took a picnic to a park near Lee's house. It was a warm day, and after they'd eaten, they lay on the rug soaking up the sun.

Jenny rolled over to look at Lee.

'You never told me about you family,' she said. 'How you came to be at Oak Hall.'

Lee didn't move, but his face seemed to darken. After a while he said, 'I don't like to talk about it.'

'Oh,' said Jenny. 'Okay. Sorry.'

There was silence for a few minutes. Jenny watched Lee's face. He was frowning and looking thoughtful. A couple of times he looked like he was going to speak, and then eventually he did.

'All right, I *should* tell you,' he said. 'If we're going to be . . . I mean, since we're together, you should know, well, everything about me, I guess.'

He paused and looked at the sky. Jenny waited patiently for him to go on.

'My parents were shot.'

'Shot?' Jenny asked, shocked. She'd meant to listen quietly, but she couldn't stop herself from asking, 'What happened?'

Lee rolled over to face her. He looked like he had resigned himself to tell her the whole story now, and was less hesitant.

'We were a typical Chinese family,' he said. 'Mum and Dad owned a takeaway. We lived in the flat above it, with my gran.' His voice was cynical, bitter. Out of character for him.

'Mum and Dad were working late in the shop one night, and me and Gran were upstairs. I'd already gone to bed, but I wasn't sleeping – I was reading comics. Gran had had this weird dream in the afternoon when she was napping, about fiery hailstones or something like that. I heard her telling my parents not to open the shop that night, that her dream was an evil omen. They laughed at her, told her that they didn't believe in superstitions and omens. They were running a business; they couldn't just close up the shop on a whim.'

He paused, took deep breaths as if steeling himself for what was coming next.

'Gran usually watched TV in the evenings, really loud so she could hear it. That night she was sitting in silence, so we both heard the noises from the shop. Shouting. Then a bang. I went down to see what it was. I was in my pyjamas. Action Man.' He smiled, a flat, embarrassed smile.

'Someone was running out of the shop. I didn't really see him, I was looking at my Mum and Dad. They were lying on the floor behind the counter. Dad was on top of Mum, like they were hugging or something. There was a tiny red hole in Dad's back; I hardly noticed it at first. I could see Mum's face from underneath him. Staring. And then I noticed the blood on the floor, pooling out around them. I just stood there, looking. And Gran came down and rang the police and I still just stood there.

'The police took photographs and measurements. And an ambulance came and took Mum and Dad away. The police asked me questions, but I was embarrassed because of my Action Man pyjamas, and I wouldn't speak to them. The police discovered later that there was money taken from the till: a few hundred pounds, I think.

'There was only one bullet fired. The police think my dad threw himself in front of my mum, but that the bullet went right through him and into her anyway. He was skinny, like me.'

Jenny lay in stunned silence as Lee told his story.

'I stayed with my gran for a while afterwards, but she was too old to look after me properly, so they took me to Oak Hall. I still visit Gran. She's in an old people's home now. I'll take you to see her one day.'

'Okay,' said Jenny, wishing she could think of something better to say.

Lee stopped speaking and looked up at the clouds, lost in thought.

Jenny lay looking at him. He *was* kind of skinny, although not in a weedy way. More lean. A fine line of soft dark hairs grew above his top lip, although his cheeks looked smooth and hairless.

She wanted to hug him. To take his pain, and use it to wrap up hers and send them both away. She wanted to help, but she felt helpless.

'I know about your mum,' he said, not looking at her. 'I read that in your file as well. I'm sorry.'

Jenny wasn't sure if he meant he was sorry about reading her file, or sorry about her mum's death. She felt a small flash of anger that he had intruded into her private world, but it went away as quickly as it had come. She was glad he knew. Glad they could share these things about each other.

'It's okay,' she said.

Clouds that had been skirting the horizon now

moved in front of the sun and Jenny felt cold. She sat up and hugged her arms.

'Did they ever find out who did it?' she said.

'Who shot my parents?'

'Yeah.'

'It was some eighteen-year-old boy. They had his fingerprints on record because he had already been in trouble with the police. He'd never shot anyone before, though. He got sent to prison. Manslaughter. Said he'd panicked, he'd never meant to shoot anyone. Said he'd broken up with his girlfriend and he was depressed. Said his parents had abused him. Boohoo. My heart bleeds for him.'

They were silent then. For a moment Jenny wished she'd never asked Lee about his parents, but then she thought, no, it was better that she knew. Better for her to understand Lee. And if it cast a dark shadow over their picnic, then so what? Some things deserved to cast a dark shadow. It wasn't good to hide from the truth, even if the truth was painful.

They were silent for quite a long time, but it was Lee who broke it.

'D'you fancy a snog?'

'What?'

"Cos I do.'

'What, here? In front of everyone?'

'Yeah.'

Jenny suddenly wanted to laugh. The gloom and awkwardness had lifted, and she lay back down beside Lee. 'Okay,' she said.

Jenny's new legs came, and she had several extra physio sessions to break them in. They were better balanced than her previous legs, and more lightweight, without losing stability. Once she got used to them, she wondered how she'd ever managed with the old ones.

A couple of weeks after she got her new legs, an American came over to meet all the kids who were involved with Project TASK, the name given to the skiing programme (it stood for Teen Amputee Skiing), and to take them for a few practice sessions at the local dry ski slope.

The American introduced himself as 'Bob'. He was enthusiastic and encouraging, and once they had got used to his American accent and expressions, Jenny and the other kids couldn't help feeling caught up in his enthusiasm. He explained about the different methods of disabled skiing, and showed them the adapted skis and 'outriggers'.

Jenny was the only double-leg amputee in the group, and Bob came and talked to her personally about her options. One-to-one he was quieter and gentler, and she felt instantly at ease with him. He watched Jenny walking on her legs, and she was thrilled when he said he thought she'd be up for four-track skis, rather than the tamer monoskis that double amputees sometimes used.

He made notes of all the equipment they would need, and a week later they met up on the local dry ski slopes. With Bob were Dr Evans and a cameraman called Andy. Dr Evans had got some extra funding from the BBC in return for allowing them to make a documentary about the project. Andy told everyone just to ignore him. At first the camera was impossible to ignore; Andy would have had more success telling everyone not to blink. But after a while they did kind of forget about it.

Jenny listened with the others to Bob giving them a pep talk, before they were each kitted out with the skis and outriggers.

She felt strange waiting to get her skis. This was it: she was learning to ski. She'd always wanted to; she'd wanted it so much that she'd killed her mother to get it. She had told herself that Eve would be glad for her, that if she didn't ski Eve's death would be wasted. But now that it was so close she wondered if she really believed that or if she was just trying to make excuses for herself.

It was her turn to get her skis fitted. Too late for second thoughts: she was here now, for better or worse. She made herself forget her worries, for now, and went and chatted to the other children.

Bob warned them that there would be a lot of falling over, and for the first half-hour at least, falling over was all anyone was doing. Jenny was paired up with a girl called Jade, who was missing her left leg below the knee. Jade got the hang of her skis more quickly than Jenny, but instead of going off down the slope without her, she stayed and encouraged her until they were both able to ski along the flat and the gentle beginners' slope.

Bob encouraged them to try a slightly steeper slope. It was still classed as easy, but to Jenny it looked like a mountain. Andy, his camera balanced on his shoulder, walked over to her and Jade as they positioned themselves at the top. If he hadn't been there, she might have chickened out, but she didn't want to look like a coward, so when Jade counted to three, she pushed off beside her.

For Jenny it was like going back in time. As if she was running again, with the wind in her hair and all the exhilaration she'd once felt pushing past other contestants around the racetrack. With her knees bent, she leaned forward, using the outriggers to steady herself. Her face was lit up with a smile she couldn't control, and she let out an involuntary whoop of pleasure. She didn't even mind that she lost her balance and fell near the bottom of the slope. She sat on her bottom, with her skis splayed out and said, 'That was brilliant!'

Jade was laughing too. She hadn't fallen, but had come to a graceful stop. She helped Jenny to her feet, and then they hurried off to do it again.

They had practices twice a week at the dry ski slope, as well as extra physio, and between that and seeing Lee, Jenny didn't have much time to read Mandy's diaries. She felt a bit differently about them now, since she discovered that they were written so long ago. She had hoped that the diaries would tell her more about the Hollands. Now it seemed that Mandy was even older than John and Helen.

She tried to spend more time with her foster family when she was at home, now that she was going out more. Playing with Stephen, or working in Helen's workshop. John remained distant, but Jenny decided that was his personality and stopped worrying about it. School was starting back in a few days. Unfortunately, Lee went to a different school from Jenny and Hayley. Jenny would have liked to have a boyfriend to show off almost as much as she would have appreciated his company.

She looked forward to seeing more of Hayley, though. She'd missed her more than she thought she would since moving out of Oak Hall.

On the Wednesday morning before school started, Helen took Jenny into town to buy her school supplies. She'd already got her uniform sorted out; Helen had brought home different sizes for Jenny to try on, as it was difficult for her to manage the changing cubicles in shops.

Shopping with her foster mother was a little awkward. Jenny knew that John and Helen were paid an allowance for her, and she could see that they were fairly well off; still, she didn't like to ask for too much. But after they'd been to a few shops and got some stationery and stuff, Helen said to Jenny, 'You know you don't have to keep choosing the cheapest of everything. You should choose things that you like.'

'Okay,' said Jenny, not really meaning it at first, until Helen covered up the prices below things and forced her to pick her favourites.

Helen was quite fun to shop with, and once Jenny had got over feeling uncomfortable, she started to enjoy it. She got everything she needed for school, and they were walking back to the car when Jenny stopped to look at a top in a clothes-shop window.

'Do you like it?' Helen asked.

'Yeah, it's cool,' Jenny said, starting to move on.

'Come on, we'll buy it,' said Helen, turning towards the shop door. 'You don't need to try it on; you could just hold it up against yourself. Come on.'

Jenny followed her into the shop, and they compared the top in the window with a few more inside, and ended up buying two.

'We should go shopping more often,' Jenny joked.

When they were almost at the car park they passed a toyshop. 'When's Stephen's birthday?' Jenny asked, looking at a display of toy cars.

Helen stared at her as if she'd said something dreadful, and Jenny took a step backwards, alarmed by her reaction.

'Why do you keep asking all these questions?' Helen said, her voice loud and angry. 'Is it not enough that we've taken you in?'

Jenny was confused and hurt. What was wrong with asking about Stephen's birthday? She just wanted to buy him a present.

'My first daughter, Lindsay, died on Stephen's second birthday,' Helen barked at her, 'and Jane died on his fourth. We don't celebrate Stephen's birthday. Does that answer your question?'

'Oh!' said Jenny. 'I'm so sorry. That's terrible. I'm sorry.'

Helen's angry expression softened, but she still didn't smile. 'Never mind,' she said. 'You didn't know.'

They drove home, and Helen went to do some work on the computer, checking her orders and emails. Stephen was still at day care, and John was at work. Jenny took her shopping through to her room, and sorted out her new things. She tried on her new tops and was pleased with both of them. She tried to decide which one to wear to go out with Lee the next day. They were going to visit his gran, so she decided against the one that said 'Sexy' on it, and went for the one that said 'Fabulous'.

When she was trying on her new clothes she noticed that her hip was hurting. She pulled down her jeans and saw that she had a bruise and some grazing. She didn't remember hurting her hip on the ski slope, but then she'd fallen so many times, she'd given up counting the places that she'd hurt.

Helen knocked at the door as Jenny was examining her injury.

'Oh, did you hurt yourself?' she said, coming in.

'Yeah, it's quite sore; I must have done it at the ski slope.'

Helen went to get her first aid kit to put a dressing on Jenny's hip. When she came back she told Jenny about some of the injuries she'd got skiing.

'I had a crush on the instructor, so I decided to show off and go on the intermediate slope. I was so busy looking at the dishy instructor that I didn't notice that the slope curved . . .'

'No!' said Jenny.

'Yes! The next thing I knew, I had crashed into a tree and was lying with my bum in the air and my legs pointing all kinds of ways. The instructor didn't even notice: he was too distracted by my school teacher, Miss Carter, who was supposed to be watching me but didn't even notice I'd fallen either.'

'What happened?'

'A fat, spotty German boy went for help. I had to be carried down the slope on a stretcher. It was really embarrassing.'

Jenny laughed, relieved that the awkwardness that she'd felt with Helen outside the toyshop seemed to have passed.

'Your top looks lovely,' Helen said. 'It suits you.'

'Thank you.'

'Jenny . . .' Helen said, her eyes searching the wall behind Jenny's head. 'I, um, I wanted to say sorry, about before. I mean, about losing my temper when you asked about Stephen's birthday. It's just, well . . .' She sighed, and Jenny could hear that her breathing was shuddery, as if she was trying to control her anxiety.

'It's just that, um, when I lost my baby girls, it was . . .'

She took a deep breath.

'It was terrible. Really terrible. I didn't want to live any more.

'My beautiful girls – gone.

'I, I literally couldn't bear it. I felt so hollow inside I

thought I would surely collapse into myself. I thought a weight was pressing me down. I thought I couldn't breathe. I thought I was breathing poison.'

Her voice was reaching a crescendo of intensity, but then she paused and was quiet again.

'It was only Stephen that kept me going. My little boy.

'They say that time heals, and in some ways it does. But some things never heal. I will never stop hurting about Lindsay and Jane. They were my future. They were the part of me that would live after I died. They were so beautiful, so full of life, and so brave. When they got ill, and their legs and arms hurt, they didn't complain, they didn't say, "Why me?" They would just lift up their arms for me to hug them, to hug away the hurt.'

Tears were falling down Helen's face, and Jenny realised that her own face was wet with tears too.

'I hugged them and hugged them, but I couldn't make the hurt go away. And they were taken away from me so I couldn't even hug them any more.'

It was as if Helen had forgotten that Jenny was there, as if she was talking to herself.

'I couldn't let that happen to Stephen. I had to take away Stephen's hurt too. Anyone would. Anyone would do ...'

Her eyes were roaming as she spoke, and as they passed over Jenny, Helen gasped and abruptly stopped talking.

'Oh!' she said, laughing a touch manically. 'I just

came to apologise, and here I am getting all emotional. Forgive me, Jenny.'

'Of course,' Jenny said. 'There's nothing to forgive.'

'Yes, well. I'll just go and get the dinner ready, shall I?'

Jenny said goodbye, and stared at the door thoughtfully after Helen had closed it behind her. What had she meant by taking away Stephen's hurt? Stephen wasn't ill like his sisters. Had Helen been about to tell Jenny about something she'd done, and then stopped herself just in time? Some secret thing about Stephen?

Ten

The new school-term started, and Jenny was amazed at the difference it made not being in her chair. She could see eye to eye with her peers for the first time, instead of having to look up to them. And they could see eye to eye with her without having to look down. She realised that the bitterness she'd felt about her disability was what had stopped her from caring about schoolwork, but now that she was happier, she began to feel the old competitive spirit rise in her again. She wanted to do well; she wanted to be the best, even. She'd chosen options for her GCSEs during the previous year, and launched into the new courses with enthusiasm.

The ski trip was planned for November, in two months' time. They were going to Austria, and Bob the American was coming with them. Two teenaged amputees from the American ski programme were coming too. Jenny was both uneasy and very excited about the trip. Uneasy because of the guilt that still gnawed at her, and excited for lots of reasons. It would be her first foreign holiday for one thing, and she'd dreamed of skiing for so long, she couldn't believe that it was finally happening. Being with other disabled people was liberating as well. It took away the 'being different' factor that still invaded so much of her life. She was already pining at the thought of being away from Lee for a whole week, though. He promised to phone her, and she promised to bring him back a gift.

But two months was still a long way off, and school-work was piling up. Jenny started doing her schoolwork on the dining-room table, with Stephen getting on with his home-schooling work beside her, but that didn't really work out. She had to clear away everything at meal times, and Stephen's chatter distracted her quite a lot. Having been an only child she was used to having peace to do her homework, and when Hayley chatted to her at Oak Hall, she hadn't minded because she did-n't really care about homework then. She tried not to complain about the situation, though, as she didn't want to get Stephen into trouble, so she just got on as best she could. It was a nice surprise then when one day John came home from work and said, 'I bought you something today, Jenny.'

She looked up at him, surprised.

'What is it?' she asked.

He lifted his briefcase up on to the table and twid-dled the combination locks, then opened the lid. He pulled out a thin, glossy booklet and flicked through it before pointing out a picture in it.

It was a desk. A nice solid wooden desk with drawers and a matching leather chair. 'For your room,' John said, sounding genuinely happy to be able to give Jenny a gift. Jenny imagined he must have loved giving presents to his daughters, before they died. 'For you to do your homework in peace.'

'Oh!' Jenny looked at the picture and then up at John, who was beaming expectantly at her. 'Wow, thank you, it looks perfect. Thank you.'

She reached over the table and gave him a half-hug with her arm.

He was a little flustered by the unexpected physical contact, and stuttered slightly when he said, 'It'll be delivered next week. I was going to wait and surprise you with it, but I'm not very good at keeping secrets.'

Jenny instantly thought of the secret of the 'paper-work' that rattled, but she pushed that thought down. John had done a nice thing and she should be grateful. She *was* grateful.

'This way I get to enjoy the anticipation,' Jenny said.

'Well, yes. That's quite right. Exactly,' said John, and then, as if the conversation was getting too much for him, he backed out of the room. At the door he remembered his briefcase and dashed back in for it, as if it might run away. After closing and locking it, he left again, saying, 'Um, well, I'll see you later then.'

Jenny smiled at the door as it closed behind him. Perhaps she'd been wrong to worry about John lying about the 'biohazards'; maybe there really was an inno-cent explanation. John seemed just like a slightly shy but nice man. The caricatured absent-minded scientist.

Helen also helped her out by letting her have free use

of her computer. She didn't seem to mind, although Jenny knew that she used it a lot to run her pottery business. A lot of the stuff on the computer was pass-word-protected, so Helen set Jenny up with her own account. When Jenny asked her why she had passwords, she laughed.

'Oh,' she said, 'Stephen once decided to go on the computer "like Mummy does". I had my business email folder open. He replied to about ten emails with little friendly messages like "Hello, I'm Stephen". I had to write to my customers and explain. Nobody minded, of course, but I realised it could have been a lot worse. I have accounts set up where I can order in supplies with a single click, or cancel orders, or all kinds of things. I've made him his own account now too, so he can access a couple of child-friendly websites and practise typing and so on. He likes the kid's encyclopaedia.'

Jenny smiled; Stephen was a boy who loved to soak up knowledge. She could imagine him poring through online encyclopaedias.

Jenny asked the hospital to rearrange her physio ses-sions so she wouldn't miss so much school. They were very accommodating, and she managed to arrange it so that she had one evening session and one session on Friday afternoons, when she would only miss PE. Lee came and met her on Fridays after her physio and they would go out somewhere. Sometimes they visited Lee's gran. She was small and frail-looking, in a nursing home that smelled of polish and old people. Her wrin-kled face lit up, though, when she saw Lee, and she started smiling just as much at Jenny, once she'd got to know her a bit. She mostly spoke in Chinese, and Jenny would listen to her and Lee speaking to each other in sounds that made no sense to her. She wondered idly if their children would speak Chinese, and would she be able to understand them? She was in a world of her own, imagining her and Lee's children when Lee's gran spoke her name.

'Jenny.'

She jumped slightly, and brought her attention back to the real world.

'Yes, Mrs Lee.' It was funny calling her Mrs Lee; it would be like calling her own gran, if she knew her, Mrs Jenny. But she was Lee's dad's mum, and Mrs Lee was her name.

She wasn't smiling at Jenny this time, but peering intently, as if she couldn't see her properly.

'I dream about you,' she said.

'Did you?' said Jenny.

'Not good dream. You live with hidden secret. Secret dragon steal your flesh. Be careful, Jenny.'

Jenny looked at the old woman, not sure whether to laugh or to feel afraid.

'Okay,' she said, 'I will be careful. Thank you, Mrs Lee.'

'That not all,' she went on. 'Second dream, this one good. Your mother, Eve, she tell me, tell Jenny she must forgive herself.'

Mrs Lee nodded and smiled, satisfied that she'd relayed her message.

Jenny stared at the old lady, who now looked as if she was nodding off. What was that all about? She didn't believe in mystical dreams – it was all nonsense, wasn't it? And yet, hadn't Lee said his gran had dreamt about his parents' shooting? Could there be some truth in what she said? 'Secret dragon steals your flesh.' What could that mean? Was there really a secret at the Hollands'? But who was the 'dragon' and how was it stealing her flesh? And then what she said about Jenny's mother. Could Lee have told her about what happened to Eve? Could the old lady have made that bit up just to make her feel better? Or was Eve really talking to her from 'the other side'? The implications were too much for Jenny to deal with straight away, but she tucked them away in her mind to think about later.

At the bus stop outside the nursing home she asked Lee about his gran's dreams.

'She's just a mad old woman,' he said, sounding angry.

Jenny looked at him questioningly. Why was he angry?

'It's not real, Jen. I know what you're thinking, that she got it right about my parents. But that was just a coincidence. The opposite of a lucky guess. Because if it wasn't . . .'

He paused and looked away from her, then down at the ground. 'If it *was* real, then I should have done something about it. She told me it would happen and I didn't stop it. If Gran's dreams are true, then I as good as killed my parents.'

'NO! Lee, no.' Jenny gently turned Lee's face so that he was looking at her. 'It's not your fault. There was nothing you could do. Even if you had known, you couldn't have stopped them. You were just a kid. They didn't believe your gran. They wouldn't have believed you either. Lee?'

He smiled reluctantly. 'S'pose. I guess we're made for each other, hey?'

Did he mean because they'd both killed their parents? But we didn't, Jenny thought, we were just kids. We didn't know. By including herself with Lee, was she really beginning to forgive herself?

She took Lee's hand and smiled at him as their bus came towards the stop.

The next week Jenny brought her ocarina into school to show the music teacher, Miss Hurst. Miss Hurst loved it, and asked her to accompany the choir on it in the upcoming concert. Jenny agreed, and took the sheet music home to show to Stephen.

Stephen looked at the music and said to Jenny, 'I can't actually read music. I might learn to some time. I can kind of guess it by looking at it, but it might not be completely right. If you tell me how the tunes go, though, I can make up the notes for you.'

Jenny sang the songs for him as best she could, considering that singing was never one of her greatest talents. He started playing along with her after a couple of lines, even harmonising with the melody.

'Wow,' she said, 'that's beautiful. Can you teach me?'

They worked together with their ocarinas for at least an hour. Jenny wrote down the fingering patterns, so she could practise later. Stephen would have kept going longer, but Jenny got tired first, and made an excuse about having to do homework.

She actually did have homework. Something about the immune system and organ transplants for biology, and a letter of complaint for English. The letter of complaint was easy: she could think of dozens of places that didn't provide enough help for disabled people. Besides, she thought cynically, the English teacher is hardly going to give me a bad mark if I write about my disability.

The weeks passed quickly, and the two months until the ski trip soon became two weeks. The choir recital was one week away, and Jenny was going to sit on a chair on the stage with the choir and play her ocarina into a microphone. She was practising a lot and feeling quite nervous. She knew the pieces inside out, but the closer she got to the performance, the worse her playing seemed to become. Helen heard her hitting a lot of bum notes, and suggested she take a break.

'Why don't you come into the workshop with me? I'm making a new batch of ocarinas today; I'll give you a lesson.'

Jenny was torn between relief at having an excuse to stop practising and worry about not being ready for the concert. But she had been looking forward to making her own ocarina, so she said, 'Okay, thanks, I'd like that.'

They went into the workshop together and sat down at the long wooden table.

Helen pulled a lump of clay out of the sack that sat below the table, and divided it in half, giving one half to Jenny.

'Now,' she said, 'work the clay in your hands until it's nice and soft. Just squeeze and knead it – yes, like that. Good.

'Now split your lump in half, and put one half down. With each half in turn, we need to make what's called pinch pots.'

Helen demonstrated with her clay, her fingers seeming effortlessly to create a smooth, even shape.

'It's very important to the tone of the whistle that the edges of the body are even,' Helen said. When she was satisfied with Jenny's pot, they worked on the other halves of their clay, trying to make them identical to the first ones.

'Good,' Helen declared after a while. 'Now, the fun part.'

She showed Jenny how to 'glue' the two halves together using watered-down clay, or 'slip'. Then they made mouthpieces.

'Look,' said Helen, 'it's really important to attach the mouthpiece correctly. If it's slanting down or up, even just a little, it'll ruin the tone of the whistle.' She reached over for a thin tool. 'Now it gets tricky.'

Jenny thought to herself that it had been tricky for quite a long time already, but she stayed silent and watched.

'This tool is to poke down the mouthpiece to make the hole that you're going to blow through. You have to make sure that the hole is level with the top of the inside of the whistle.'

Jenny looked at her lump of clay and wondered if she should give up now. 'How can I tell if it's in the right place?' she asked, her voice sounding anxious, as she probed with the tool.

Helen smiled. 'Don't worry,' she said, 'you can always start again; that's the beauty of clay, remember? Wiggle it about a bit to make the hole slightly wider, but be careful to keep it level.'

Jenny did so, and then handed the tool to Helen.

'Looks good,' she said, and quickly bored a hole in her own mouthpiece.

'Now we make an opening exactly where the mouthpiece joins the ocarina.' She demonstrated with hers first, and then watched Jenny. 'You should be able to make a nice even tone now, if you blow down the mouthpiece.'

Jenny picked hers up and blew tentatively. A smooth, deep note came out.

'Whoohoo!' she said.

Helen laughed. 'It's good,' she said. 'Much better than my first attempt, but then you have a great teacher.'

Jenny nearly wanted to stop with that one note and not bother with finger holes, but Helen told her not to be such a chicken.

'The problem with tuning an ocarina,' she said, 'is that the notes we get now will not be the same as the notes it makes after it's fired, because firing the clay shrinks it.

'So, we have to make the note a little bit too flat to begin with. Luckily for you, I have so much experience in making ocarinas that I can tell when it will sound right, and as my apprentice, I'll pass that great skill to you.'

Jenny bowed slightly, as a good apprentice should.

They made holes of different sizes. Helen explained that in an ocarina, the size and number of holes was all that mattered; it didn't matter where you put them, except that some positions were more comfortable to play.

After they were satisfied with the range of notes, they added hoops of clay so that the whistles could be threaded on to strings and worn as pendants. Then they were finished.

'So, Jenny, you made an ocarina.'

'Yeah,' said Jenny, looking at the clay instrument, 'I did.'

They washed up the tools and their hands, and Helen moved the ocarinas over to a tray of things waiting to be fired. Jenny looked around the shelves of finished pieces while she did.

She lifted some and saw that Helen had signed the bases.

'Why are some of the pots signed 'HH' and some signed 'Helen Stone'?' she asked.

'Oh,' said Helen. 'Well, after I'd been selling stuff for quite a few years I thought people might be getting bored of Helen Holland pieces, and so I started a new range under my maiden name, Helen Stone. I thought Stone was quite a good name for a potter.'

'It is,' said Jenny. 'But you can't have been selling things that long; didn't you used to work as a scientist before you had children?'

Helen suddenly looked annoyed, but she kept her voice light and said, 'Jenny, all these questions, you're worse than Stephen! But I can explain, of course. My pieces are quite expensive, and so are bought by the rich and fashionable. Fashions can change very quickly. That's all. No mystery.'

'Okay,' said Jenny, wondering why Helen was so upset by her innocent question. That was something unsettling about Helen. She was friendly and nice most of the time, but little things could set her off and she would suddenly become angry. Jenny remembered when she'd nearly dropped a knife on Stephen (okay, she thought, Helen had good reason to be angry then) and when she'd asked about Stephen's birthday (again, though, Jenny thought that Helen's anger was reasonable enough, considering). Even the time she asked Helen about sending Lee back. She'd got quite upset then. But then she's only human, and everyone has faults in their personalities, Jenny reasoned – if it even was a fault at all. And she had lost two children in the last three years. Enough to make anyone borderline hysterical. Still, it made Jenny a little nervous around Helen. As if she was walking on thin ice.

The night of the concert came around, and Jenny was so nervous she could barely dress herself. Lee had come for dinner so that they could all go to the concert together. But Stephen developed a bit of a cough, so John volunteered to stay at home with him.

Jenny had to go backstage when she arrived. She said goodbye to Helen and Lee, and joined the choir. A girl in her class called Andrea came in just after her and said to the room at large, 'Who's that gorgeous Chinese guy? Did you see him?'

'Oh,' said Jenny casually, 'that's my boyfriend, Lee.'

She could almost hear the surprised reaction around the room and felt herself buoyed up by the new sense of admiration.

'I thought your boyfriend would be . . . well, you know . . . disabled.'

Jenny turned to the girl who'd said that, and fought down an urge to hit her.

'Oh no,' she said, 'Lee's all there all right.'

This brought laughter and Jenny joined in. One of the gang.

Soon it was time to take their places on the stage. Jenny went and sat in her seat, where she held her ocarina ready while the shuffling died down and the curtain was opened. She was so nervous that her hands shook and her mouth felt like sandpaper. She took a couple of steadying breaths and waited for her nod from Miss Hurst. She had to play first, an introduction to the choir, who would join in after a few bars and then she would play a harmony over their voices. She caught Lee's eye just before she got her cue from the music teacher, and she smiled at him as she lifted the whistle to her lips.

From the first note she played she forgot her nerves, forgot even that she was being watched, and just lost herself in the music. She even managed to trill the notes the way Stephen had patiently tried to teach her. The sound of the ocarina with the voices of the choir was beautiful. In practices they had hardly ever played the piece all the way through without stopping and starting, and when they had there had always been shuffling or coughing. Now the only sound was the music and it was magical.

When it was over, the audience clapped and cheered and Jenny bowed from her seat. For a moment her smile faltered, as she wished Eve had been there to see her – but she had Lee, and Helen, and Hayley was there with her foster family too. She smiled again as the curtain closed, and just before it hid the audience, she almost thought she saw Eve clapping and beaming with the others.

Eleven

The next few days were spent busily getting ready for the trip. Packing and checking passports and last-minute adjustments to her legs. Jenny was trying to get ahead with her schoolwork as well. She asked the teachers to give her the work she would miss in her week away, and she tried to get most of it covered before she left.

She still found time to paint her ocarina, though. She wanted it to look like her memory of the day she spilt the beads, when she was little with Eve. She remembered the colour of the carpet – blue –– and the colours of the beads, or at least the fact that there were lots of colours. In the end the ocarina looked a bit funny and spotty, not as good as she'd hoped, but then glazing improved it and she was pleased enough with the finished product. She dedicated it to Eve, in a sort of silent inner ritual. She thought Eve would have approved of that sort of thing.

The ocarina was the last thing to go into her suitcase the night before the trip, along with the photo of her and her mum. She kissed the picture before putting it in.

'I'm sorry, Mum,' she said, and she really meant it. The picture smiled back at her, and she felt peaceful. As if Eve was accepting her apology and showing her forgiveness.

She zipped up her case and made sure she had everything she needed in her hand luggage: tissues, her purse, a magazine, some sweets, a drink, her camera. She opened the drawer in her bedside table and pulled out the last two of Mandy's diaries. She hadn't even thought about them for a while, but they just popped into her head. She thought she might as well read them, if only to pass the time on the coach. That done, she got into her pyjamas and went through to the kitchen for her cocoa. She brought it back to her room and sipped it in bed. She wanted to get to sleep quickly because it would be an early start in the morning, and she thought that she'd be too excited to sleep. She needn't have worried, though: sleep took her soon enough.

The hospital car park was eerily deserted in the early morning chill. The night-time dark was lifting, but there was no spectacular sunrise on the city skyline, just a gradual lightening of the sky. The small crowd of young people and their parents didn't need sunrises to lift their spirits, though. Teeth were chattering with cold and excitement, but everywhere faces were smiling. Suitcases and crutches lay in jumbled heaps, as last-minute inventories were taken. Andy took it all in with his camera, which by now the children really didn't notice.

Jenny stood with John, Helen and a sleepy Stephen. He had begged to be allowed to come and see Jenny off, even though she had to be at the hospital at five-thirty in the morning.

Even in his sleepy state, Stephen still managed to be chatty. He babbled on about what Jenny was going to be doing. He wanted to know all about her route to get to Austria, and which countries the coach would be driving through. Jenny said she would buy him post-cards if the coach stopped on the way, and that she would get him a present from Austria.

Stephen asked her if Austria was the country where everyone was upside down.

'No,' said Jenny, laughing, 'that's Australia, and they're not really upside down there.'

'I know really,' said Stephen. 'Because of gravity and space and stuff. It's funny, though, isn't it?'

'Yes, it is funny.' Jenny looked at Stephen's smiling face and wondered at what a special little boy he was. He was clever and he knew a lot more than you would expect a five-year-old to know, yet he was funny and mischievous, and vulnerable. She wanted to pick him up and hug him, to tell him how special he was.

Just then the coach pulled up, and everyone was dis-tracted by loading up the luggage. There were packed lunches provided by the hospital canteen (Jenny could only imagine what they would be like) and boxes full of juice cartons for the trip. Jade, the girl who Jenny had befriended at the dry ski slope, was there with her par-ents. She saw Jenny and came over.

'Hi!' she said. 'Jenny, I'm so excited.'

She turned to John and Helen. 'You must be Jenny's parents,' she said. 'Hi, I'm Jade.'

It didn't occur to Jenny that Jade didn't know she was in a foster home, although when she thought about it she realised she just hadn't mentioned it. It was an innocent enough mistake, but it made Jenny feel funny. As if she was being disloyal to Eve.

'This is my foster family,' she said. 'John, Helen and Stephen.'

'Nice to meet you,' said Jade, not reacting to learning that Jenny was fostered.

'Can I sit with you on the coach?' she said. 'I don't get travel sick.'

'Yeah,' said Jenny, smiling, 'of course.'

The largest suitcases belonged to the two American kids, introduced to the group as Leticia and Brad. Leticia was a double above the knee amputee like Jenny, the only other one she'd ever seen, and she couldn't help staring at her a bit, seeing what others must see when they look at her. Brad was a single amputee like Jade, missing one foot.

'He's gorgeous,' said Jade, looking over at him.

Jenny tore her eyes away from Leticia and gave Brad an appraising look. 'He's all right,' she said, 'if you like the skater-boy look.'

'Well, as of now I do,' said Jade.

The girls giggled, and had to look away suddenly as Brad sensed he was being watched and turned around.

Finally it was time to get on the coach. Jenny hugged

Helen and Stephen, and shook hands with John. Dr Evans was helping everyone on to the vehicle. Jade followed Jenny, and she grabbed her as she lost her balance.

'That would be a great ski trip if you broke your arm getting into the bus,' she said.

'Well, at least I can't break my leg,' Jenny quipped.

'Nobody is to break any legs,' said Dr Evans, partly joking and partly serious. 'Those legs cost a lot of money.'

When everyone was finally on the bus, they waved out of the windows at the parents. John lifted Stephen up so he could see to wave at Jenny, which he did with both hands until the bus was out of sight.

'Your foster brother's cute,' Jade said to her.

'Yeah,' said Jenny, realising how fond she'd become of the little boy. 'He's lovely.'

It didn't take very long to drive to Dover, or at least it didn't seem long. The roads were fairly clear and the bus was full of excited chatter. They had to wait for forty-five minutes at the ferry terminal before the coach drove on to the boat, but even that went by quickly.

On the ferry they had to go up in the lifts in shifts, and then they all congregated at a seating area. Jenny found it very difficult to walk on the boat. The rocking movement of the floor was making even able-bodied people stumble, and it was more than she could manage. She ended up staying in the seating area for pretty much the whole time. She did make one trip to the toilet, though. She overheard a mother telling her children that they should use the disabled toilet because there was always a queue in the normal ones. She had to stifle a laugh as the mother rounded the corner to see fifteen teenagers on crutches waiting outside the disabled loo.

The coach drove along the border between France and Belgium, and Jenny looked out of the windows at the passing fields and towns. She couldn't help thinking of Eve, travelling through Europe. Did she travel on this very road? She wondered if Eve had picked grapes in the fields they passed, if she had walked in the meadows of flowers, or had drunk wine in the taverns and inns that looked so picturesque.

They had a stop in Belgium and Jenny dutifully bought a postcard for Stephen. They ate their hospital canteen lunches, which were surprisingly good, in Luxembourg. Jenny bought another postcard and local stamps, and quickly sent the two cards to Stephen. She bought a card for Lee too, but waited to take more time over writing it later.

After lunch the bus rolled on. They had to pass through Germany before they got to Austria, and finally the chatter died down as everyone started to get sleepy.

Jade rolled up her coat as a pillow, and leaned her head against the window. Jenny tried to sleep too, but found she couldn't, so instead she took out Mandy's diaries.

She looked inside the covers to see which diary to read first. Mandy wrote the day and the date on her diary entries, but not the year – but as she always began her diary on her birthday, it was easy enough for Jenny to see which was which. The first diary Mandy wrote began when she was ten, then eleven, and then twelve, so Jenny selected the one that began when Mandy was thirteen.

Friday 9th January

This is the diary of Amanda Jean Patterson, aged thirteen and three weeks. I couldn't begin this diary on my birthday because of what was happening then, but boy, do I have a lot to tell you now.

Firstly, I finally got away from my evil scumbag Dad. He's back in prison where he belongs. He got caught robbing a bar. He had a drink first, so they got his fingerprints off the beer glass, HA HA!

Secondly, my mum had a kind of breakdown. She was dead stressed out with all the Dad business. Like his partners in crime coming to our house all the time and hiding their loot there. And her and Dad fighting all the time. And I don't just mean the things they screamed at each other. The hitting was getting worse. Not that she didn't give as good as she got, and at least when she was hitting Dad she didn't hit me so much. When the police came and arrested him, I thought, great, it'll go back to just me and Mum and we'll be happy again. But she fell apart. She was crying and hugging Dad's clothes and stuff all the time, as if she really missed him. She must be mental. Who would miss him?

And she did start hitting me again. Just for nothing. Like she said, 'Pick up your coat from the floor,' and I said, 'I'll pick it up later,' and she hit me for it!

I don't think she's a bitch or anything, 'cos she's my mum, you know, and I love her. It's my Dad's fault. He got her all uptight.

It was kind of scary, what happened. Because my mum just lost it. I was walking home from school with Alison and some other girls, and Karen Walker said, 'Isn't that your mum in a nightie?'

I couldn't believe it. Mum was staggering down the street, outside the chippy, and everyone was coming home from school, so everyone saw her. And she was wearing her old tatty nightie, not even her nice new one. And she was crying so much that her mascara was running down her face so she looked like a zombie from beyond the grave. And Mrs Theophilus from the chip shop came out and invited her in for a cup of tea. I was so embarrassed, I didn't go into the chip shop to get her, I just went home. Then she didn't come home for hours, and I didn't know what to do. But later on, at about nine o'clock at night, these two women came to the door and said Mum had to go to a psychiatric hospital and that I should pack some stuff and they would take me to be looked after.

Jenny paused in her reading. Jade was snoring gently beside her. In some ways she felt she could empathise with Mandy. Even though their backgrounds were very different, there were some things they shared. Like being mostly brought up by their mums. Like loving their mums, but being embarrassed by them at the same time. Not that Eve had ever had a breakdown. She was a bit loopy, but at least she was stable and consistent in her loopiness. Jenny didn't know what she'd have done if Eve had lost control. Jenny had felt safe with Eve, in spite of all her idealism. Eve had been remarkably sensible and level-headed about some things. Like always making sure Jenny had clean clothes and healthy meals and that she brushed her teeth and did her homework.

In a strange way Jenny was glad that she was in care because Eve had died, and not because she'd been unable to care for her, like Mandy's mum or Hayley's mum. She would always know that Eve had been there for her. Had loved her.

The sky outside the coach windows was dark now, and the windows became like mirrors, reflecting back Jenny's face as she tried to peer out. She opened the diary again and read by the glow of the little overhead light.

I took my clothes and a few other things. I felt funny with those women in the house - I didn't know how long I would be away or how much to pack. I had a look in Mum's wardrobe. I don't know why I did. Well, actually, I do. I was looking to see if Mum had bought me a birthday present. At first I thought there was nothing there, but then I saw a pink envelope with 'Mandy' written on it. I grabbed it and brought it with me.

They drove me off to Princes Road Children's Centre. I asked the women if it was a home for bad children.

One of them said, 'No, of course not, it's just a place for you to stay until your mum gets better.'

They took me in and this woman, Mrs Parker, filled in loads of forms and stuff. I felt weird. Like, what's going on? This morning I went to school as normal, and this evening I'm in a children's home. Mrs Parker said most of the children were in bed already, and she would introduce me in the morning. She said I could sleep in the overnight room to begin with, but they'd get me a proper bedroom in a day or two. I said there was no need because I'd be going home. Mrs Parker looked at me like, poor dear, she thinks she's going home. I felt angry. I don't know why, but I felt like shouting. I did shout. 'You can't keep me here!' Mrs Parker didn't shout back, she just stayed calm and stood up. I thought she was going to hit me, so I ducked, but she didn't hit me. She put her arm around my shoulders, and said, 'Sleep on it, and see how you feel in the morning, okay?'

Jenny remembered how she'd felt arriving at Oak Hall. Scared, unsure, but at least she'd had time in the hospital to get used to the idea. It must have been terrible for Mandy, for everything to happen all of a sudden like that.

I went to bed but I couldn't sleep. It was quite late, but not as late as I sometimes go to bed. The room smelled of paint and polish. The bed was funny. It didn't feel right. I went and looked out of the window. It had bars over it, like a prison. I asked Mrs Parker about that the next day, and she said it was a safety measure, so children don't fall out, because the windows open really wide. The bars made shadows on the wall in the night. The light from a street-lamp shone through the window, and if cars passed, the shadows moved across the wall. I could hear noises, clankings and hummings, and little scraping sounds. It was scary. When I did sleep I had bad dreams. I dreamt that I was in prison with my dad, and he turned into a rat, scurrying around the floor. And he jumped on my face, and I screamed. I woke up and there was a rat, or I thought it was a rat, on my face. It turns out it was a hamster. This little boy came running into my room, calling, 'Hammy, Hammy! Where are you?' And he grabbed the hamster off me and said, 'Oops, sorry,' and ran out again.

You know how weird it is waking up somewhere

strange? Well, that's nothing to waking up somewhere strange with a hamster on your face. Now that's weird.

Then a woman came and told me to get up and get ready for breakfast. And then she took me downstairs to meet the other kids.

I didn't know how to be when I walked into this room full of kids. They were all sitting around a long table having breakfast, and they looked up at me. And I didn't know if they'd all be really hard, or if they'd hate me, so I just sort of looked at them. And then this girl moved up and said, 'Come and sit here,' so I did, and it was all right. They're not really hard. Apart from this girl called Fiona, who looks like she'd stick a knife in you given half a chance. But most of them are just kind of normal.

So most of the kids went to school on that first day, but I didn't. They said I could have a day off school while we sorted things out, so at least that was one good thing to come out of it. I was really embarrassed thinking about going back to school. Everyone would be talking about my mum. Alison would stand up for me. But no one else would.

They moved me into a bedroom with the girl I'd sat beside at breakfast – Sharon. She's all right. She's a bit pink and girly, but she's nice though.

It was my birthday two days after I arrived

at the home. I didn't tell anyone, so I didn't think anyone would know. I woke up early, and I slipped my hand under my pillow to where I'd left the card from my mum. I pulled it out and I don't know why but I wanted to cry. Before I even opened it. Sharon was sleeping, so I sat up quietly and slid my finger under the flap so it would open without tearing. Something tinkled inside it, and when I pulled out the card there was a necklace in the envelope as well – a silver necklace with a heart on it. I put the necklace on and read the card. It said, 'To a special daughter on her birthday'. Mum had written inside it: 'Happy birthday Mandy, my little angel. Love from Mum.' Not 'Love from Mum and Dad' – just Mum. I put the card back under my pillow and lay back down until Sharon's alarm went off.

That was three weeks ago and now it seems almost normal living here. Some of the kids went home for Christmas, but lots of us stayed. I even got some presents from the staff. I asked Mrs Parker if I could go and visit my mum, but she said I should wait a while longer until Mum was feeling better. She asked if I wanted to visit Dad in prison. Ha, I said, no thanks.

Well. That's enough writing now. It's really late and Sharon's snoring as usual. See you tomorrow.

Jenny closed the diary as if she was coming up for air. They were in Germany now and the coach was pulling into a service station for petrol. Dr Evans asked if anyone wanted to visit the toilets. People shook away sleep and stretched out necks and arms. Jenny didn't really need the toilet, but she wanted to buy a postcard for Stephen, so she got off the bus with the others. It was dark and chilly, and Jenny wrapped her coat around herself. When Dr Evans handed her her crutches, they felt cold in her hands. She fumbled in her pockets for her gloves, and felt a small plastic rectangle. She pulled it out and looked at it. It was a picture of Lee in a cheap plastic frame. He'd given it to her on their last evening together before the trip. He'd insisted that the photo was terrible, but Jenny thought he looked stunning in it.

'Who's that?' Jade was looking over her shoulder.

'That's my boyfriend, Lee,' Jenny said, grinning.

'Cool, he's cute,' said Jade. 'Does he have all his legs?'

'Jade! You're as bad as the girls at my school. Yes, he has all his legs and arms and any other bits you might want to ask about. He's an orphan, though, like me.'

'Oh. Were you in a home together?'

'Yeah, but we're both out in foster homes now.'

Lee told her before she left that he had finally found out why so many foster parents had sent him back to Oak Hall. He'd asked Sarah about it and she'd apologised, said it was her fault really. She said that because Lee was so nice she had sent him to families who hadn't fostered before, to break them in gently. She said she hadn't given enough thought to how it would make him feel. Jenny remembered how hurt Lee had been by the apparent rejections, and wished he'd thought to go to Sarah sooner.

Everyone was out of the bus and sorted with their crutches by then, so they gladly went inside the service station.

Jenny bought a card and a stamp for Stephen, and quickly wrote and posted it, and before long they were back on the last leg of the journey.

Twelve

Everyone was awake, and the last hour and a half passed with wild raucous singing. They were half-way through 'Ninety-nine artificial legs hanging on the wall' when the bus pulled up outside their hotel.

The hotel looked quaint and picturesque, like a giant cuckoo clock uplit by strategically placed yellowish lights. Snow-covered mountains lined the sky behind it, glowing in the moonlight like a painted movie backdrop. Jenny could hardly believe that they would soon be skiing down them. It was late, but the hotel was expecting them and had a room ready for their evening meal, once everyone was checked in and the luggage had been taken up to the rooms. Jenny was sharing with Jade and two younger girls, and she didn't even mind that they had to share two double beds between them.

The room beside theirs was taken by the two female chaperones on the trip. One was a physiotherapist named Sheila who Jenny knew well from her sessions at the hospital. The other was a nurse, and although Jenny didn't remember meeting her before, she was instantly likeable, and had the air of someone who could cope with anything. As well as those two and Dr Evans, there were three other adults in the party. One was Bob the American, one was another doctor, who Jenny vaguely remembered from around the time of her accident, and the other was Andy, the documentary maker, complete with his camera and sound recording equipment. He taped the singing on the bus, and set up a projection screen in the dining room so they could watch a montage of clips about themselves to the soundtrack of their own crazy singing. Jenny saw herself laughing along with the others. She looked happy. Even shots that showed her removing her legs didn't look grotesque to her, just normal.

Dinner was a sort of meat stew with dumplings followed by a selection of delicious cakes and pastries and coffee or cocoa. Jenny ordered cocoa, relieved that she would not have to go without what had become a part of her bedtime ritual. As they nibbled the last of the cakes and sipped their drinks, Dr Evans and Bob went through the itinerary for the next day. They would start with breakfast, followed by a session of adjustments that had to be made to the prosthetics. Artificial limbs behave differently in cold weather, but the doctors were prepared for that and had brought heat pads and other things to sort them out.

After that session, they would hit the slopes, the part they'd all been waiting for, then lunch, then more skiing, then dinner and hanging around the hotel until bedtime. Dr Evans mentioned the open-air hot tubs as a fun way to spend the evening. Brad and Leticia whooped, but the other children looked uncomfortable. Jenny had packed a swimsuit – it had been on the list sent to her from the hospital and Helen had bought her one specially – but she didn't intend to be seen in public wearing it. Even though she'd worn shorts at Oak Hall, she still didn't feel comfortable with people seeing her body, especially strangers, and there was something about a swimsuit that made her feel especially deformed. Maybe it was the contrast between herself and the gorgeous swimsuit models from magazines or beauty contests. She remembered a friend she'd had at her old school, before the accident, who had been horribly embarrassed to be seen in a swimsuit because she was overweight. Jenny hadn't really understood how she'd felt then, but now she did.

They made their way back to their rooms, tired but still excited. Craig, the boy Jenny got to know in her physiotherapy sessions, was whispering with another boy, and they nodded and giggled to each other.

'What are you boys plotting?' said the nurse, who had told them all to call her Cathy.

Craig jumped and looked decidedly guilty, but managed to squeak, 'Nothing.'

'Yes, well,' she said, 'it had better be nothing, because there's not much that gets past me. Okay?'

They scurried off. Craig had left his foot with Dr Evans for a minor repair, and he was swinging his footless leg vigorously to help him speed off on his crutches. The other boy was wearing an artificial lower leg, but struggled to keep up with Craig. Cathy chuckled after them, as if she would in fact happily let them get away with a lot more than she was letting on.

The girls in Jenny's room quickly brushed their teeth and got into their pyjamas. Helen had bought Jenny warm fleecy pyjamas that were soft and snug, although a little too warm for the heated hotel room. She rolled up the legs and used safety pins to hold them in place over her stumps so that they wouldn't get tangled up in bed, and then sat talking to the others. One of the younger girls, a small blonde called Abigail, was missing both arms from just below the elbow. She was amazingly dextrous with the residual arms and brushed her teeth holding the toothbrush between her elbows. She had special artificial arms that would hold her ski poles, with a quick-release mechanism that she could interchange with her other prosthetic arms. Despite her angelic appearance, Abigail was a very tomboyish and mischievous little girl, and she had all the other girls in stitches with her jokes and impressions of Dr Evans and Bob the American. They were laughing so much that it was a while before they realised that they were hearing noises from outside.

There was a clattering, accompanied by subdued but approving whispers. Then an excited cry of 'Yes!' and a loud crunching sound. The girls decided to go on to the balcony to see what was happening.

Two balconies over from theirs was the room that Craig and the other boy were sharing. Underneath the boys' balcony snow had piled up in a drift, and Craig was lying spread-eagled in the snow laughing and saying,

'Yes! Brilliant!' The other boy was poised on the balcony ready to jump down after him.

The girls shivered in the cold but stayed to watch anyway. The boy jumped, arms and legs splayed, and landed in the snow with a crunch.

'Wicked!'

He turned over in the snow, waving his arms about and making strange, mutated snow angels as he did. 'Hang on a minute,' he said. 'Oh no! Where's my foot? I've lost my foot!'

Some more heads had poked out of balconies by now, and children began shouting encouragement and advice.

'Is that it? There, look . . . Oh no, that's a Coke can.'

'Where were you when it fell off?'

'What does it look like?'

'What does it look like? What do you mean, what does it look like? It looks like a flipping foot!'

Abigail had gone back into the room, and when she came out again she was carrying one of her arms tucked under her armpit.

'Help me down,' she said to Jade, who lowered her with some difficulty over the balcony. She started digging about in the snow with her prosthetic arm, using the hand like a shovel.

'I've got it!' she yelled triumphantly, lifting a white frosted foot and lower leg out of the snow. 'Oh, blast, now I've lost my arm.'

She found the arm quickly enough, but then she and the boys realised they couldn't climb back up to the balconies.

Jade tried hauling them all up, but she couldn't reach so well, or get a good grip on Abigail's arms. Finally an amused voice from the next balcony said, 'Oh, come over here, I'll pull you up.'

It was Cathy the nurse. She pulled up Abigail and the two snow-jumping boys, and sent them off to bed with threats of telling Dr Evans, 'who would have every right to send them home'. Jenny heard her laughing to her roommate, the physiotherapist, though, and saying, 'Why shouldn't they get up to high jinks like normal kids? Goodness knows they have enough to put up with.'

After all the excitement had died down, they turned out the light and settled down to sleep.

Jenny could soon hear the other girls breathing deeply and occasionally snoring. She heard other noises too: the distant rumble of hotel trolleys bringing clean linen or room service to guests about the hotel, the rise and fall of traffic noises, engines approaching and departing. Once she heard laughter outside the door to their room: laughter and muffled chatting which, like the traffic noise, rose and fell as the happy people, whoever they were, came closer and then passed the room. It struck her suddenly that the others had been asleep for quite a long time and she was still awake. She looked at the luminous hands on her watch. Two-thirty. She felt wide awake. She thought that she'd moved beyond the insomnia that had troubled her in the hospital and at Oak Hall. She'd had no trouble sleeping at the Hollands' – so why couldn't she sleep now? It was too dark to read, and she didn't want to risk waking the others by turning on the light. Instead she slipped herself out of bed and on to the floor. She crawled on her stumps over to the balcony windows and sat looking out. It was cooler by the window and Jenny was glad of her fleecy pyjamas. Hugging her arms around herself, as much for comfort as for warmth, Jenny sat and thought. She thought about Lee, and those thoughts made her smile and tingle deliciously. She thought about Eve, and wondered if she lived on somewhere; if her immortal soul left her body and moved on, waiting for Jenny to join her one day. She hoped so. It seemed ridiculous to believe otherwise, that Eve could have been nothing more than just nerve impulses and chemical reactions. That she could end and be just a body decaying in the earth. She hoped that Eve was watching over her and that she *had* sent a message to her through Lee's gran. She smiled and hoped Eve could see her. I'm trying to forgive myself, Mum, she thought. I think I can, if you can. And then a new thought came to her and she spoke it with her inner voice. I think I can forgive my dad too now. Gilberto. Maybe I'll look for him when I'm a bit older, so he can see what I've grown into. Yes.

Then she thought about Mandy, about her being in care, about her being a strange mixture of vulnerability and resilience. I suppose we all are, she thought. We cope, but we worry. Whatever life throws at us, we keep going, keep moving forward. We worry about the future, when the future could surely not treat us any worse than the past. Well, me anyway, she thought. If you'd have asked me two years ago what's the worst that could happen, I might have said death or terrible injury, and look, they happened. And look at me. I'm okay. I coped.

She thought about Helen, making her beautiful ceramics and raising her son. Moving on with life. Because life was worth living. Even after all it had thrown at her, she still thought that.

She didn't know how long she sat, but eventually her eyes began to droop and she pulled herself back into bed.

In the morning she felt as if Jade was pulling her up from a deep, comfortable tunnel. She heard her calling, 'Wake up, Jenny, come on, wake up!' She felt as if she had only just entered the deepest part of sleep and didn't want to leave it yet.

'Jenny! Wake up!'

'S'all right,' she managed to say. 'I'm awake.'

She yawned through breakfast and the session of adjustments to limbs and crutches. It wasn't until she was standing with the others in the white light and cold air of the mountains that she felt fully awake. The view was breathtaking. When the shuttle bus had collected them from the hotel the sky had been overcast, so that the white mountains had blended with the white sky and it was hard to see where one ended and the other began. But by the time they arrived, the sun was shining and the clouds had burned away. The sky was the brightest blue that Jenny had ever seen, and the jagged tops of the mountains looked sharp as scalpels in contrast. Everywhere there was white snow with patches of black rock or trees, and Jenny thought it looked like a giant Friesian cow was lying across the landscape. Pretty wooden cabins were dotted about, some with snow still lying heavily on their sloping roofs and others newly melted clean in the morning sun.

The sun warmed them, even though the air was bitter. They had sunscreen on their noses and Jenny felt silly, and then she laughed that her white nose was embarrassing her more than her lack of legs. There were other people using the ski slopes: families and couples, beginners laughing nervously, more experienced skiers boasting to their friends about which slopes they'd conquered. Brad and Leticia were giving a pep talk, because they were experienced disabled skiers. Leticia demonstrated turning and stopping, and herringboning to climb up the slope. Jenny again watched her raptly, her ease of movement and confidence inspiring her.

'Right,' said Bob the American when Brad and Leticia had finished, 'are you guys ready for the experience of your lives?'

Smiles and nods came from the group of kids. Bob was not impressed.

'What, are you all still asleep?' he said. 'I said, are you guys ready for the experience of your lives?'

'Yeah!'

'Whoohoo!'

'Bring it on!'

'Wicked!'

'That's more like it.'

The kids were separated into more skilled and less skilled, and the better ones went off with Bob and Leticia to a more advanced slope. Brad stayed with Jenny's party, much to Jade's delight.

'Now, guys,' he said, moving himself over to the top of the slope, 'when you stand right here –' He paused dramatically. '– and look down the mountain at all the little biddy trees and people, you are the king (or queen) of the world. All it takes,' he went on, looking them all in the eye in turn, 'is for you to lean forward, just enough, and you're off! Speed gods. Snow dragons. And that split second, as you move your weight forward and wait to let gravity take you, is the best damn moment in your life. Jenny!'

'What? Me?'

'Yeah, you – how many gorgeous girls called Jenny are there up here?'

'She has a boyfriend,' Jade blurted out, then instantly blushed almost purple.

'Well, he's a lucky boy,' said Brad.

He made Jenny come to the top of the slope, and poise herself beside him.

'Now, lean forward,' he said.

She did, looking down at the world below her. She felt like she was at the top of a cliff, or about to step off the edge of the world.

'Feel the fear,' Brad was saying in her ear. 'Feel the excitement. Feel how alive you are.'

Jenny felt her insides twisting with anticipation.

'Now go!'

She leaned her weight just a little bit further, and she was off!

Sliding. Falling. Flying.

She almost forgot all the form she'd been taught as she felt the sheer joy of speed. Just in time she remembered to steady herself with the outriggers, to lean her body this way and that, holding her legs at angles that wouldn't have been possible with her old prosthetics. Tears streaked down her face from the wind or the emotions that threatened to engulf her. Who would have thought that Jenny could do this? She remembered her dreams of crawling on her stumps through endless rooms.

'Sod you, dreams!' she shouted into the wind. 'Look at me! I'm not crawling any more!'

And then she was at the bottom, and she managed to stop without falling. And her breath came in shuddering gasps between exhilaration, exertion and laughter.

She remembered the poem she'd written: 'I wonder if I'll find myself, and snow and cold will be my home.'

'Yes!' she said. 'Yes.'

Then she felt for a moment that she wasn't alone, that Eve was with her, smiling. 'Thank you, Mum,' she said quietly. 'Thanks for everything.'

Jade joined her then, and they got the ski lift back up together, an experience almost as alarming as skiing down.

Again and again they skied down the slope, and when Bob came back to tell them it was time to return to the hotel for lunch, Jenny couldn't believe the time had passed so quickly.

After lunch they were back to the slopes again, and by the time the minibus took them back to the hotel for dinner, Jenny was exhausted.

Dinner was hearty and warming, just what they needed. Again, Andy the cameraman showed footage that he'd shot during the day. He was an experienced skier himself, and was able to ski backwards while filming. The shots he'd taken were in parts inspiring and beautiful, and sometimes just plain hilarious. He seemed to have an uncanny knack of being there with camera rolling whenever anyone did something spectacularly embarrassing, like falling bum over heels or missing the ski lift. He also captured some great moments: graceful skiing, looks of triumph. Jenny imagined that when the whole thing was put together it would be very cool. She wondered, with a bit of a thrill, whether it was going to be shown on TV. Eve had been in a TV documentary when she was protesting against something or other – why not her?

After dinner, Dr Evans told everyone to get into their swimming things and meet at the hot tubs. Everyone started squirming in their seats and a low rumbling mumbling filled the air like a distant avalanche. Jenny said to Jade, 'You go if you want, but I don't want to.'

Leticia was sitting on the same table and she overheard.

'Why not?' she asked.

'I just don't, um, feel comfortable, you know.'

'Oh no,' Leticia said, 'you just don't want people to look at you. But let me tell you, you are gorgeous, and people should look at you and do their eyes a favour. And if you want to feel comfortable, a hot tub is the place to be, umm humm. You ain't felt nothin' until you've felt those hot bubbles, girl.'

Jenny felt for a bizarre moment as if she was on the Oprah Winfrey show or something. Though she did feel inspired by her disability twin.

'Okay,' she said, 'I'll do it.'

As if encouraged by her bravery, others said they would come too, and in the end all the children congregated by the hot tubs, to the astonishment of the other hotel guests. Arms and legs were left by the side and everyone climbed in. Under the bubbles disabilities were forgotten, and the aches and weariness from the day's skiing were eased by the hot water.

Cathy and Sheila sat at a table near the jacuzzis, sipping drinks. They shouted encouragement to their young charges, and brazenly ignored the curious or even disapproving looks from the people around them.

Later, wrapped in a towelling robe and sipping cocoa, Jenny felt as happy as she had in ages. She was exhausted too, and thought that she would surely not have trouble sleeping that night. She was frustrated, though, when she went to bed: she still waited restlessly for sleep, and wondered, before finally drifting off, if she should ask Helen to take her to the doctor about it when she got back home.

Thirteen

The rest of the week went by in a blur. They had a coach trip to a picturesque village where they could shop or sit in cafés drinking coffee. Jenny bought a T-shirt for Lee, a little crystal swan for Helen, some chocolate for John and a snow globe for Stephen that had a tiny skiing figure inside it with arms that moved at the shoulders. They had another trip to see a castle one day, and the rest of the time was spent skiing. Cathy and Sheila were kept busy massaging sore muscles, and even the doctors got roped in to do some physio work.

When it was time to pack up and go home, everyone was sorry to leave. They were going to travel overnight, leaving Austria early evening to arrive at Calais the next morning. Jenny made sure she took Mandy's diaries in her hand luggage, as she knew she wasn't good at sleeping on the bus.

As they drove away from the hotel, Jade chatted to Brad, who had the seat behind theirs. She'd been trying to get close to him all week, but he only seemed to notice her on the last day, which made her scream with frustration when they talked about him at bedtime.

She insisted she would get his phone number by the end of the coach trip, and Jenny smiled to herself as she listened to her attempts.

Jenny felt slightly guilty about eavesdropping, so she tried not to listen. She decided to get Mandy's diary out and read to distract herself from their conversation.

She read for an hour, not noticing Jade turning back around and settling herself down for a sleep.

Mandy's short stay at the children's home turned into a long stay. Her dad was going to be in prison for at least five years; he had an appeal, but it failed. Her mum got out of the psychiatric hospital and went back home, but she didn't take Mandy back. She explained that she loved Mandy, but she couldn't cope with being a mum, and she hoped Mandy understood.

Mandy's feelings about her mum's decision fluctuated hugely. Some days she seemed to be fine about it:

I can understand why Mum didn't want me to go home. She wants what's best for me. Like here I've got good food and enough clothes and stuff, and nobody is hitting me. She comes and visits me and that's good. I know she's lonely without me but she's doing the right thing anyway.

Other times Mandy sank into depression and anger:

I must be so horrible that even my own mum doesn't want me. Alison went off with Karen Walker, the miserable cow. Just 'cos I said her new skirt made her look fat, and it did. I suppose

I shouldn't have said it, though. That's just like me. Opening my big gob and putting my foot in it. That's probably why Mum doesn't like me. Why nobody likes me. Who could blame them. I'm stupid. Stupid, stupid,

Most of the time, though, she just got on with life. Her diary was filled with day-to-day stuff. New children at the home, things going on at school. She finished the fourth diary and closed it. One more to go. How would the story end?

Almost everyone on the bus was sleeping now, even the adults. It was like Jenny had wandered into Sleeping Beauty's castle. She almost expected to see vines and ivy growing over people. The bus driver was awake, of course, but he didn't count, lost as he was in his own world of changing lanes and looking for exits. Jenny stretched and looked around. She noticed that Craig was also awake in the midst of a sea of sleepy heads. He was reading a comic, and he stopped and looked up, as if he sensed that he was being watched. She caught his eye and smiled. He smiled back, but his smile looked sad and Jenny suddenly wondered what was going on in his head. Everyone has their problems, I guess, she thought.

She turned around again and wondered if it was worth trying to get to sleep. Although she was tired, she felt alert, restless even. There wouldn't have been room to walk around the bus, even if she had the balance of an able-bodied person, and they were unlikely to have a rest stop any time soon. She wondered if her newly returned insomnia was physiological – although that didn't really make sense, as her life was getting better, not worse. Maybe she should talk to her counsellor about it anyway. She sighed and rummaged in her bag for the next one of Mandy's diaries. She may as well read it to pass the time, she thought.

It started off much as the previous one had finished: Mandy still in the home, the same sort of things annoying her or making her happy. Jenny almost felt herself starting to get drowsy, until she read something that shocked her back to full wakefulness.

It was about a third of the way through the diary; that is, about four months after Mandy's fourteenth birthday. Mandy had been told by Mrs Parker that she was going to be fostered. She went through many of the emotions that Jenny could identify with: shock, excitement, anxiety, fear, and also a sense of satisfaction at being chosen, of being wanted by someone – a spark of hope that there might be something about her that people would like, even love.

Jenny felt empathy welling up inside her as Mandy agonised about what she should wear to meet her new family, what she should say, how she should behave, how to stop herself from ruining everything as usual. But it was what she read next that really shocked Jenny.

Thursday 21st April

Today I finally got to meet the family that are going to foster me. They are a Mother and Father, with a little boy called Stephen, who is about five years old. They took me to the park, and we fed the ducks, and I pushed Stephen on the swings. He's a really nice little kid. He never stops talking though! The mum and dad are called Mr and Mrs Holland, but they said I should call them John and Helen.

At this point Jenny nearly dropped the book as she gasped in surprise. John and Helen Holland with their son Stephen? What was going on? It had to be the same John and Helen; it was too much of a coincidence otherwise. But how was that possible? Mandy's diaries were thirty years old. At least, that's what the letter in the box they dug up had revealed. But they couldn't be. Was Jenny the victim of some elaborate joke? Had Mandy been fostered only weeks or months ago, and was the buried box staged to look older than it really was? But why would Mandy pretend to have lived thirty years ago? And why had the park changed since she made her map? Unless she just made that up.

There was no way that Mandy could have been fostered with John and Helen in the 1970s; Stephen would be grown up now, John and Helen would be old. Could there be another family with the same names? Relatives of the John and Helen from now? It was possible, but no! History doesn't repeat itself like that exactly. It just didn't add up, whichever way you looked at it. Jenny floundered in a sea of 'what ifs', not sure whether to be angry, or confused, or amused, or all three.

She wished Lee was there to talk to. He would think

of some explanation, wouldn't he? Or at least she could bounce her ideas off him. Not that she really had any ideas – nothing that added up anyway. It just didn't make sense.

She was still less than half-way through the diary, so all she could do was read on.

John didn't say much, not like my real dad who never shut up. He was nice with his son though, like he was really happy to be at the park with him, and it wasn't a big bore for him. I liked that, that's how a dad should be. Helen was nice too. She says she makes pottery, and she'll let me help her. Wow, I'm really excited, although I'm rubbish at art so I'll probably just make a fool of myself.

They were a bit sad too. Mrs Parker told me that they had two little girls that died, so I suppose they would be sad. It makes me worried though. What if their girls were really nice and cute and good, and when I go and live with them they'll expect me to be like that, and when I'm not they'll hate me and send me back?

They showed me their house on the way to the park. It's really nice. Down its own private lane through a wood, like some rich person's mansion or something. I can't believe I'm gonna live there. I could have Alison around for tea and she'd be dead jealous. Except that she's still going around with that cow Karen Walker.

She might want to be my friend again if I lived there though.

I have to start packing my stuff. I'll miss Sharon, it'll be weird not sharing a room any more. I wish she could come with me. I asked Mrs Parker, but she said they only try to keep real brothers and sisters together, and that Sharon's only my roommate, and that I'll not miss her too much when I get settled. I know I never had any brothers or sisters before I came here, but I've kind of got used to being around other kids. Still, there'll be Stephen. Even though he's only little, he might be fun to be with.

I've got to do my homework now. I'll still be going to the same school, worst luck. Maybe I could persuade the Hollands to move house.

Jenny read quickly through the next few days' entries, impatient to get to the bit about Mandy arriving at the Hollands'. Mandy hadn't written much anyway, and most of it had been repeating her feelings of anxiety and excitement about being fostered.

Then she found the day she'd been looking for.

Sunday 1st May

Well, I'm here. Stephen gave me the tour of the house. Upstairs the two girls' bedrooms are made up as if the girls were still alive – all pink and frilly with dolls and stuff. It's kind of creepy, but I guess it's understandable. They only died a

196

year or two ago. I suppose it would be too painful for John and Helen to pack up all their stuff and throw it away or whatever. John and Helen's room is upstairs as well, but my room and Stephen's room are downstairs. My room is lovely: all blue and yellow and really big. My window looks out over the brilliant garden. Oh, yeah, the garden's really big. There's a stream and everything. It's like living in the park. One of the big trees has a rope swing on it, and a wooden ladder up to a tree house. That's so cool.

Rope swing? Tree house? Jenny wondered why she hadn't noticed those things in the garden. If Mandy was fostered recently, wouldn't they still be there? Maybe they took them down before I came, she thought, because I couldn't use them. Still, it was strange. She could have used a rope swing, and Stephen could still have used his tree house. Never mind.

She looked at the diary once more:

Helen made me cocoa to take to bed. Cocoa! I've never had it before. It's nice, hot and chocolaty (well, it would be). I'm keeping my diaries in the drawer beside my bed. I have a big beanbag in my room and that's where I'm sitting now writing.

It's really cosy. I could go to sleep. In fact I

The day's entry ended there. Jenny turned the page to the next day:

Monday 2nd May

Can you believe I fell asleep in the beanbag last night? I must have got up in the night and got back into bed because I woke up in bed, even though the last thing I remember is sitting writing my diary.

I must have been lying on my pen because there's a red mark on the inside of my elbow like the pen has made a hole in it. I don't know what is in the ink of my pen but the mark is really itchy, and a bit sore, and I couldn't wash it off.

Helen showed me her workshop. It was brill! She's so talented. All these gorgeous things she's made like plates and pots and jugs and things, and she signs them all with this ace curly double H, for Helen Holland. I'm practising a groovy signature like that, although AP doesn't work quite so well as HH. She makes these weird musical instruments as well – ocky-somethings. Stephen was trying to play one, bless him. It sounded all squeaky and out of tune. He seemed pleased with himself, though, and said he was going to practise loads and get even better. Well, I thought, he couldn't get much worse! I wouldn't say that to him, though, he's a real sweetie. When he curled up in my lap with his blanky it made me want to have babies of my own. Yeah, I know, I'm only fourteen. I'm not a total idiot – I don't want to have babies yet. Not that I even have a boyfriend. Not that Peter is ever going to notice me. Will I ever be Mrs Welshman?

The next two pages at least were taken up with drooling over Peter Welshman and moaning over how he didn't fancy her. Jenny felt impatient with Mandy, and quickly skim-read it, eager to get back to hearing about John and Helen, searching the text for clues about what was going on. That comment about Stephen's ocarina playing, for instance. Either Mandy had no ear for music, or she was with the Hollands before Stephen learned to play well. But his playing was brilliant, and sounded like he's been practising for years, and yet Mandy said he was five years old and hopeless. It just didn't add up. She wondered how much she should trust the things Mandy had written – after all, she didn't know her and she had obviously had a rough life. Maybe the diaries were full of lies, things she'd just made up. That could explain all the things that didn't make sense. Jenny was beginning to feel scared, though. What if Mandy wasn't lying? The implications were too mind-blowing to take in.

Saturday 14th May

Today I made a pot. Helen showed me how to do it with the potter's wheel and everything. She gave me this weird lecture about how brilliant clay is, like clay is this amazing stuff and all the things that you can make from it. It was pretty amazing, though, making a pot on the wheel. Much better than those tiny pots we made by wrapping big clay snakes round and round in primary school. I'm going to paint it next week, after it's been fired. I wanted to see the kiln, which is in this sort of basement room underneath Helen's workshop, but she wouldn't let me down there. She made some dopey excuse about how it's really untidy down there or something – like I would be upset by a bit of mess, considering what my mum's house used to look like. I'll ask her again tomorrow. I bet she'll give in in the end. It's not like I'm gonna burn myself or anything – I mean, I've done cooking in school, and we've used dangerous machines in woodwork and metalwork. She's just used to having really young children, I suppose, and having to protect them from stuff. That'll be why.

Stephen had his friend Johnny round for the afternoon. The two of them were like a couple of puppy dogs or something, running around the place and tumbling over each other. Helen was getting really uptight about it. She kept looking at them through the window and gasping if they fell over or something. I could tell she was trying to stop herself from going outside, but eventually, when the boys were taking it in turns to jump down from the tree house, she did go out and made them come in and sit at the table and have a snack.

Then it was time for children's television, so I sat with the boys and we watched *Hong Kong Phooey*. Then Johnny's mum came and took him home, and Helen seemed to relax a little bit.

When John came home, Helen went out to meet him in the hall. I didn't mean to listen in on them, but I happened to be going to the toilet, and I stopped when I heard them talking.

Helen said, 'Did you manage to get a microscope from the lab?'

John said, 'Yes, one of the old ones from the storage cupboard in C lab.'

'And did you get the stains as well?'

'Yes, all of them.'

Then they started saying all kinds of things I couldn't understand about chromosomes or something, and it sounded like they wanted to make something, like some kind of a machine that would stop contamination, and John said he could bring home some stuff from the lab where he works, and they said something about it being disastrous if something happened to the tissue cultures.

I had no idea what they were talking about, but they looked really cross when I came out of the toilet, like I'd caught them cuddling in the nude or something. They got all flustered and John had this big coughing fit. Helen didn't lose her cool so much, though, but she looked at me really funny, like she was weighing up how much I'd heard. I wouldn't have thought twice about it if they hadn't reacted so strangely. Now I'm a bit freaked out.

It's like they've got this big secret, and I don't know what it is and I don't know if I should be afraid.

Jenny felt at once justified and terrified by what she was reading. If she had suspicions about John's biohazards and Helen's phone conversations about running tests, and Mandy had overheard that strange conversation between John and Helen about microscopes and chromosomes and tissue cultures, then there must be something going on. Something secret.

But what was it?

Could it be something to do with Stephen? Sarah had told her that the Hollands' girls had died of some kind of genetic disease. So maybe Stephen had it too; maybe Stephen would die without whatever it was his parents were doing. She remembered Helen saying she had to take away Stephen's pain, that day in her room. And when the doctor visited, didn't Helen tell him that Stephen had started his new treatment? But why was it such a secret, and what did it have to do with her or Mandy?

Fourteen

Mandy's suspicions weren't mentioned for a couple more weeks in her diary. She just went back to talking about school and Peter Welshman and life with the Hollands; it was like she'd forgotten the overheard conversation. Until she overheard another one.

She'd started the day's entry with something else that immediately aroused Jenny's interest, although Mandy obviously hadn't attached any significance to it.

Friday 3rd June

I don't feel so well today. I woke up with a sore throat and a sort of burny pain in my chest, and I've been burping up yukky stuff that burns the back of my throat. I told Helen and she let me have the day off school and stay in bed. I don't seem to have a fever or anything. I don't even feel that ill really. Just a bit sore. It's kind of boring actually, being in bed. All the days I wished I was in bed instead of at school, and now I nearly wish I was at school instead of in bed (ha ha). Helen's in her workshop, I think, and

John's at work, and Stephen's at his nursery school. I'm bored. There's not even somebody to play I-Spy with!

I think I'll go and look for Helen.

Oh my gosh, now I'm really scared. I went to find Helen, and she wasn't in her workshop, but the door to the basement was open. I thought that if I called her she'd come up, but if I just went down, then I'd see whatever mess she'd been hiding down there and then she'd have no excuse for not letting me see the kiln. So I snuck down the stairs to the basement, but before I got down, I heard Helen talking. I thought she must have someone with her, but then I realised she was talking on the phone.

Jenny felt goose-bumps forming as she read about Mandy's experience, which so mirrored her own.

I listened to what she said, and then I had to get the big dictionary down from the shelf in the living room to be able to understand the words, let alone spell them.

I'm normally not very good at remembering stuff, especially not complicated stuff, but somehow her words are like burned into my memory. I think this is what she said:

'I've got the cells that we harvested from Mandy's oesophagus. I extracted the undifferentiated cells and I'm starting a culture now.

I'm going to try those first two growth mediums, the ones that worked best with Stephen's cells.

'Yes, I think we should try them both.

'Well, because we don't know enough yet to know which will have the best long-term effect. They both stimulated the production of the cell types we need, but there were small differences. Let's try them both, yeah?

'Yeah, Mandy's feeling a bit sore today. Must be from the endoscopy – she thinks she has a throat infection. I let her stay off school. She'll be fine in a day or two, then we can get some more cells if we need to. The blood cultures seem to be doing okay as well, and then there's always bone marrow – I've been reading up about biopsy techniques. We should be able to get those easily enough too. I don't think we'll need brain tissue at all.

'Yes, from the hip.

'I know, I think it's really going to work.

'Yeah.

'Yeah.

'I love you too.

'Bye.'

I tiptoed back up the stairs and then ran into my room. I don't think she heard me. When I went back out for the dictionary there was no sign of her.

So I've been looking up the words, right, and it means they've been taking cells from my food pipe that are 'undifferentiated,' which means 'Having no special structure or function; primitive; embryonic', whatever that means, and growing them in a tissue culture, which is just some way of growing cells outside a human body. The endoscopy is putting a tube down my throat and looking into my insides so they could scrape cells out. I feel doubly ill now thinking about it. They've been scraping cells out of my food pipe while I was asleep. I can't believe it. I don't know what to do.

They must have been taking blood from me too. That's what the hole in my elbow was, not from some stupid pen. I don't like the sound of a bone marrow biopsy either – that means sticking a huge needle into my hips and sucking out bone marrow.

And what about brain tissue? She said, 'I don't think we'll need brain tissue.' But what if they do? Are they going to open up my head or something?

I'm really really scared. I don't know what to do.

Jenny let out a big breath she didn't realise she'd been holding.

Whoa – this was more than just hints and suspicions. The phone conversation that Mandy overheard was much more specific than the one she heard – Mandy actually overheard Helen saying that they'd taken cells from her. 'Undifferentiated cells' – something in Jenny's mind clicked when she read that. Was it something she'd done in biology? No, she remembered now. It had been on the news a few days before she left for Austria. A news report about stem cells. Stem-cell research. As far as Jenny understood it, there were cells in a baby's placenta that could become any type of cell, like a bone cell or a skin cell or anything, and scientists could use them to replace cells in a person with a disease, like people with Alzheimer's disease could grow new brain tissue with these stem cells. The news story was about a family who wanted to have a baby so they could use its placenta to help their sick child. They couldn't just get pregnant in case the new baby had the same disease, so they had to use IVF. The problem was with the screening of their embryos: they would be picking embryos specifically to suit the child they wanted to treat. There was a big ethical debate over it. Phrases like 'designer babies' and 'playing god' were thrown about in discussions, while the parents watched their child get sicker. But the news report had said they needed placental blood cells. Jenny wasn't a baby, and she certainly wasn't pregnant, so the Hollands couldn't be looking for placental cells. Were there stem cells in teenagers? There must be, Jenny thought: that's what Mandy overheard – they'd taken undifferentiated cells from her oesophagus. Stem cells.

Jenny felt cold and wrapped her cardigan tightly around her.

She looked back down at Mandy's diary.

They must be drugging me at bedtime, so they can do their medical stuff on me at night. It's the cocoa. It must be. I always go to sleep really quickly after my cocoa, and I sleep really deeply.

What'll I do with my cocoa tonight? If I drink it I'll be drugged and they'll be able to do stuff to me. But if I don't and they come for me in the night, how could I explain why I'm not asleep? Or what if I go to sleep anyway, but then I wake up in the middle of some medical procedure? Oh no Oh no Oh no.

Jenny was beginning to wonder the same thing. Would it be better just to let herself be drugged than to pretend to be asleep? She didn't want to wake up to find the Hollands scraping cells out of her. It made sense to her now why she'd had so much trouble sleeping on the ski trip. Her body had got used to having sleeping tablets or whatever every night and now she couldn't sleep without them. It was like when they weaned her off painkillers in the hospital. She didn't know whether to feel relieved or just angry. Angry and scared.

The more time Jenny had for what she was reading to sink in, the more anxious she felt. She was trembling now, trembling and feeling sick. She saw a sign for Calais flash past the window, driving the icy knife of fear deeper into her. The bus was taking her back to them. Back to the family that were using her as a human lab rat. What should she do?

Helen just brought me my cocoa. She smiled and said she hoped I was feeling better. I wanted to scream and run away. I wanted to throw the cocoa back at her. But how could I? She would only have to call for John and they could hold me down and force me to drink it.

'Can I get you anything else?' she asked. So sweet and caring.

'No thank you.' I tried to sound sweet back, but my voice was shaking.

'Are you all right, love?' she said. Love! Huh.

'I'm just missing my mum,' I said.

She believed me, I think. She leaned over and hugged me. 'Don't worry,' she said. 'We love you.'

Yeah, I thought, you love 'harvesting my cells'. 'Thank you,' I said. 'I love you too.'

I looked to see if there was any guilt. Any worry or uncertainty in the way she looked at me. But no. She just smiled. Like the cat who got the cream.

I took a sip of the cocoa. She watched me, then left.

I'm going to drink it. It's better than facing them in the night.

I'd rather be asleep thank you very much.

Tomorrow I'll think of a plan.

Maybe I'll go to the police, or at least to Mrs Parker.

But would they believe me?

The word of the troubled teenage daughter of a criminal father and a Loony Toon mother, against the word of the lovely smiley Holland family. I don't think so somehow.

I only took a tiny sip of the cocoa. I'll drink the rest when I've hidden my diary. I can't risk John and Helen finding it. There's a loose floorboard under my bed. I'm going to hide my diaries there.

I can already feel the effect of the cocoa.

No one's going to believe me, are they?

They'll think I'm just making trouble.

They'll think I'm a bad girl.

My mum will cry and say, 'Now do you see how she drove me to madness?'

My dad will laugh and say, 'Now do you see how she drove me to crime?'

I'm hearing noises outside my room. I'd better hide the diary quickly and then drink my cocoa in case they come in.

That was the end of that day's entry.

Jenny turned the page. There was only one day's entry left to read, then blank pages. It wasn't the end of the year. Why had Mandy stopped writing?

Monday 6th June

I think they know that I'm on to them.

The writing was bigger than usual, messier, like she'd written it in a hurry.

I'm probably just being paranoid, but I'm sure that there's an atmosphere in the house. They're looking at me strangely, I know they are. And giving each other meaningful looks behind my back, I see them when I turn around. And they stop talking as soon as I walk into a room.

They know.

I'm sure of it.

And I'm really scared.

Who knows what they're capable of?

What they would do to protect themselves.

I've got to get away.

I've got to escape.

Tomorrow is the Queen's Silver Jubilee, there's going to be a street party. There'll be lots of confusion, lots of people. I'll go then. They'll not realise I've gone for ages. I could hitch-hike.

They'll never find me.

At least I pray to God they won't.

And that was the end.

Jenny scanned the blank pages, praying for some sign, some clue.

WHAT HAPPENED NEXT?

The Queen's Silver Jubilee. Silver is twenty-five years. How long has the Queen been the Queen? Jenny tried to remember. She'd studied the Queen's coronation in history. It was ages ago. But how long ago is ages? Mandy, where are you? What happened to you? Did you get away? Did they catch you? Did they kill you?

Could Helen and John be murderers?

With these thoughts bombarding her mind, Jenny was too caught up in her feelings of panic to notice that the coach had pulled into the ferry terminal at Calais, and when Dr Evans stood up and called out to wake everyone, she jumped and gasped.

Beside her, Jade was stirring and stretching, almost elbowing her in the face. The bus began to hum with chatter, and Dr Evans had to shout to be heard again. He told them they had an hour before the coach had to board the boat, and they could get off and go to the terminal building to use the toilets or buy a drink.

The complicated business of getting everyone down the step and sorting out everyone's crutches began again, and by the time they were ready to enter the building, Jenny had her anxiety under control. Then came the queuing outside the terminal's single disabled toilet. Jade was talking to Brad again, so Jenny just stood and watched the world go by. It was very early in the morning, but still the terminal was busy with people waiting for the boat: young families with excited children, backpackers looking dishevelled, a busload of football fans sleepy and subdued. An old man was helped to a chair by one of his younger companions. He looked confused, as if he didn't know where he was.

It was her turn to use the toilet, so she turned away from the old man.

Then she sat with the others, drinking Coke and joining in the chatter. Pushing down the panic into a corner of her mind. Delaying the point where she would have to do something about it. She wondered about going to Dr Evans and asking him for help, asking him to protect her from the Hollands. But what would she tell him? That she read things in a child's diary from thirty years ago? He wouldn't believe her. She didn't know if she believed it herself.

Before long they were on the boat, then back on the coach in England.

For Jenny, time was running out.

And then, before she knew it, they were back. The coach pulled into the hospital car park, where the little band of friends and family waited to welcome home their loved ones.

There were John and Helen, and Stephen holding up a painting saying 'Welcome home Jenny' and smiling so much his face could hardly contain it.

When she saw them, Jenny suddenly thought that Mandy's diary must be all nonsense. How could she have believed all that stuff? Stealing stem cells? I mean, look at them. They looked like a nice normal family. How could she have imagined they might have murdered their former foster child? She thought of John buying her a desk, and Helen teaching her to make ocarinas. Those weren't the actions of murderers, were they? She smiled and waved through the window of the bus as it came to rest beside the waiting crowd.

Everybody piled off the bus, exchanging hugs with

each other and with their anxious parents. Luggage was unloaded and phone numbers exchanged. Jenny noticed Jade getting Brad's phone number, and made the okay sign behind his back. Jade grinned at her before turning her attention back to Brad, who surprised her by kissing her on the cheek.

The bus driver came off the bus carrying a handful of random objects that had been left on seats or in the luggage racks.

He shouted out what they were and waved them above his head until the people who left them came and claimed them.

'Amanda Patterson!'

Jenny suddenly froze, and so did Helen and John.

'Amanda Patterson, you left your diary, love. Don't want the boys reading that, do you?'

The bus driver was waving Mandy's diary in the air. Jenny must have left it on the bus. How could she have been so careless? She couldn't believe this was happening. Helen and John were both staring at the diary as if transfixed. Jenny didn't move. Like a deer caught in headlights, she was powerless to do anything.

'Jenny!' shouted Jade, going and grabbing the diary from the bus driver and bringing it over to Jenny. 'Jenny! Are you blind or deaf or something? This is your book that you're always reading. Here.'

'Thanks,' Jenny mumbled, clutching the diary to her chest.

She lifted her eyes tentatively and saw that John and Helen were both staring at the diary in her hands, and then their eyes rose and met hers, and in that moment they all knew. It was true. It was all true, and Jenny knew it now, and they knew that she knew.

'Come on, Jenny! Let's go home! Mummy, Daddy, let's go home! Did you buy me a present, Jenny? Did you, did you, did you? We missed you, Jenny. Mummy made a cake and I wrote 'Jenny' on it in icing, because you were away and you came back. It's chocolate cake because that's my favourite. Do you like chocolate cake, Jenny? And the icing is white with pink writing because pink is for girls and you're a girl, Jenny. Except you know that you're a girl already.' Stephen thought that was very funny and started giggling.

Jenny looked at him and she was torn in two with emotion. She loved him. That was definitely true, and yet he was the reason for her fear. He was the reason for the Hollands doing what they did to her, and to Mandy. If she went to the police, or told anyone, would they be forced to stop treating him? Would doctors and ethics experts debate the pros and cons of the treatment while Stephen got sicker? Would Stephen die, like Eve, because of her?

But if she didn't tell, would the Hollands trust her? Could they live with the threat of her telling? As much as she loved Stephen, they must love him so much more.

Enough to kill for him?

Maybe.

She couldn't even run away. Oh, the irony. The girl who ran like flowing water couldn't run at all, now that she needed to.

'Let's go home, Jenny,' said Helen, not smiling.

John lifted her bag into the boot and Helen helped her into the car, and then went around to strap in Stephen.

Stephen wanted Jenny to tell him all about the trip. She began to tell him, her voice thin and shaky. John and Helen joined in, asking her questions, even laughing. This is not real, she thought, as she told them about the boy who lost his foot in the snow, and about Abigail digging it up with her arm. Then she described her skiing and almost forgot the bizarre circumstances as she remembered the exhilaration.

'Wheee!' shouted Stephen. 'I want to go skiing. Can I go skiing, Mummy? Can I, Daddy?'

'One day, Stephen,' Helen said.

The car pulled into the driveway of the Hollands' beautiful house. There were balloons tied to the front door, and a second banner welcoming her home.

Jenny felt like she was in a play, and that Stephen was the audience. She had to convince him that she was happy, that she was glad to be home. John and Helen were actors too, playing off each other's cues. They brought in Jenny's bag and the presents were ceremoniously given. Stephen loved his snow globe, and begged John for some of his chocolate. They had lunch. Party food laid out festively with the cake as the crowning glory. The food tasted like sawdust to Jenny, but still she ate, and smiled, and swallowed.

After lunch Stephen was put down for a nap.

And then they were alone.

Fifteen

'**So,**' **said Helen,** returning from Stephen's room, 'Mandy left a diary.'

Jenny said nothing, just nodded.

'What did she say?'

'Oh,' said Jenny, trying to sound nonchalant, 'just stuff, y'know. Nothing really.'

'Don't lie to us, Jenny,' Helen said quietly.

'Don't lie to you?' Jenny felt anger welling up inside her. It had been desperate clutching at straws to try to play innocent, to act like she didn't really know what was going on, but still she had thought it was worth it. Now, ironically, she felt irritated that they didn't take her words at face value, even though she never really thought they would.

'Don't lie to you?' she shouted, then lowered her voice when Helen looked anxiously in the direction of Stephen's room. 'Why shouldn't I lie to you when you've been lying to me all along? When you've been using me. Literally! You want the truth now? Okay, I'll tell you the truth. She said you drugged her. With cocoa. Sound familiar? She said you took her blood and you scraped cells out of her oesophagus. She said you grew her cells in tissue culture. Stem cells, except she didn't call them that. But that's what they were, isn't it? That's what this is all about. You're fostering children so you can farm their stem cells.

'And she said she was going to run away, that you knew she knew, and that she had to escape. She said she was afraid of you. Afraid of what you might do to her. And it looks like she was right to be afraid, doesn't it? What *did* you do to her? Did you kill her? Did you hide her body? Maybe you burned it in your kiln, or chopped it up in whatever kind of underground lab it is you have under your lovely home. Maybe that's what you're going to do to me now. Why are you even bothering to talk to me? It's not like I can run away, is it? You chose well when you chose the crippled girl for your latest cell bank. Is that why you chose me? Is it? And I thought you liked me, that you liked my face or something about me. How stupid was I? All you wanted was a sitting duck. Someone you could exploit. Someone that nobody would care about, that nobody wanted. Why not? It's not like I have parents who love me like you love Stephen, is it? It's not like I'm any use to anyone, is it? Except you. That's it! I've found my calling in life.'

There was bitter irony in her voice.

'Farm animal.'

'Jenny, no . . .' It was John who spoke then. Jenny looked up at him and saw the lines of pain etched into his face. 'It's not like that, Jenny. You make us sound like, like monsters. You don't understand.'

'What don't I understand? Tell me. Tell me, John.' She was almost pleading, genuine curiosity mixed in equal measure with her terrible fear. At least if they were going to kill her, getting them to talk would give her some precious extra minutes of life, and she really did want to know what was going on.

John had been standing, but now he sat down. He buried his face in his hands, and when it emerged again, Jenny was shocked to see tears spilling from his eyes.

'Helen was already pregnant with Stephen when Lindsay got sick,' John began, his voice so quiet that Jenny had to strain to hear him. 'Lindsay was just a baby herself – well, a toddler I suppose. She was so full of life. "Into everything" as they say. She used to take her toys apart to see how they worked. She'll be a scientist, that one, we used to say. We were so proud. Our perfect little family. Lindsay, Jane, another one on the way. But ... but she was always falling over. Well, little ones do, don't they? We never imagined ...We had to take her to casualty three times in as many months ... little accidents – a broken arm, a sprained ankle, a banged head. They investigated, thought we were hurting her . . .' His breath came out in a choked sob, as if the memory of the accusation still hurt him deeply. 'But one of the young doctors had an idea,' John went on, reigning in his emotion. 'He thought to do a blood test on Lindsay.

'"I'm very sorry, Mr and Mrs Holland," he said when the results came back, "but I'm afraid there's more to Lindsay's injuries than just normal toddler clumsiness."'

'I'm very sorry', thought Jenny, remembering being

told about her amputations. If a doctor starts a sentence with those words, you know you're in trouble.

'She had a genetic condition affecting her nervous system. A gradual breakdown of motor skills, and then other things: sight, hearing, thought processes. We watched our baby unravelling in front of us. When most children are learning new skills, she was losing the ones she already had. She was so frustrated – she couldn't hold her little toys any more, she had to go back to wearing nappies. "But I'm a big girl," she said.'

Again John sobbed and rubbed his face with his hands. Helen was still standing, and she hugged herself and rocked slightly as she listened to John speaking.

'They tested Jane's blood, and Stephen's when he was born. They both had the defective genes. All our babies would suffer the way Lindsay was suffering. All our babies would die.

'I was working on embryonic development, on what made certain cells in the early embryo develop one way and certain cells another. How a ball of cells becomes a baby. Helen's expertise had been in tissue culture, in growing cell lines in the lab. We read everything we could about genetic disease, all the journals, but in those days gene therapy was unheard of. The only use of stems cells was in bone-marrow transplants for patients with leukaemia. But we were sure there must be something we could do. Some way we could use what we knew about the amazing process of human development to save our children. We broke into the lab I was working in, at night, used our own blood to begin with, to see if we could isolate undifferentiated cells. It was groundbreaking stuff, but we worked with a passion born from desperation. And we did it. We found cells from the blood and from the digestive tract and from bone marrow that could be changed, manipulated into something different. But our own cells were no use: we both carried the gene for the disease that was killing our children. I applied for permission to carry out human trials. But it was turned down – or at least it might just as well have been. They wanted years more research and animal testing before they would let us use human tissue. But we didn't have years. Every day that went by was making our children sicker. Lindsay died. Jane was already showing symptoms. We knew we were on the brink of finding a treatment, but bureaucracy would have robbed us of the speed we needed.

'We set up a lab at home, and continued to work secretly on our own cells, perfecting the process. Then Jane died, and we only had Stephen left. Time was running out fast. Helen had the idea to foster. Young people with healthy cells. We could take cells harmlessly; there was no need for anyone to know. A little blood, a few cells here and there. Nothing that would harm the children – they probably wouldn't even notice.

'The first few children we fostered proved to be incompatible; their cells were rejected by Stephen's body. Mandy was the first match.

'She was right about the cocoa. We put sleeping tablets in the cocoa, increasing doses as her body got used to it – and yours too, I'm afraid.'

Jenny had been so taken up in the story that she'd almost forgotten her own involvement. Hearing about her drugged cocoa brought it back with a vengeance.

'The lift outside your room goes down as well as up. You need a key to make it go down; we couldn't have the foster children, or Stephen for that matter, wandering into the lab.

'We brought the sleeping children down in the lift. The procedures were always very quick and simple. Getting the cells was the easy part; making them become what we wanted was where we ran into problems. We tried different media, different chemicals to treat the cells. It looked as if it was working, but there were all kinds of variables, little differences in cell lines. We just didn't know whether they would affect the treatment or not. And there wasn't time to test them all, or people to test them on, so we had to take a gamble. What did we have to lose?

'We injected treated cells into Stephen, and waited with baited breath.

'There were some side effects. Lethargy, a little nausea and dizziness. We didn't know what was normal, so we had to ride it out. Our friend, Dr Jo, agreed reluctantly to monitor Stephen's health. We'd been friends since school, and I loved him like a brother.'

Jenny remembered Dr Jo's visit. But that man had been old, maybe thirty years older than John and Helen.

'Stephen recovered from the symptoms, and we tested his co-ordination and reflexes. They had improved!

We were overjoyed. It looked like the treatment was working.

'We took more cells from Mandy so that we could set up as many cultures as possible. Some cells we froze with liquid nitrogen, others we kept growing in the lab.

'Then . . .'

John's voice petered out, as if he couldn't bring himself to say what came next. He looked at Helen, as if silently asking her to go on. She nodded slightly, and then sat down beside her husband.

'There was a sudden change in Mandy's behaviour. She became jumpy, anxious. We immediately thought that she must have found out what we were doing to her. John and I didn't know what to do. We didn't think that what we were doing was so bad, but would she think that? And if she told the police, what would happen? At best they would make us stop and Stephen would die. At worst, Stephen would die, and we would go to prison. Although for me I was only concerned with what would happen to Stephen. If Stephen died, I would want to die too – what would be the point in living?'

Now Jenny's fear deepened. She could see why John and Helen would not want Mandy to tell anyone, and Helen had just told her how very strongly she felt about it. So, Jenny thought again, what happened to Mandy?

Helen went on: 'It was the Queen's Silver Jubilee. Mandy went into the village to the street party. When she'd been gone for a couple of hours, John and I felt anxious. We left Stephen with Jo and we went looking for her.

'We couldn't find her in the village. We asked some of the locals, and one or two remembered seeing her earlier, but not for some time. We were terrified that she'd gone to the police. We wondered about running away ourselves. Then we met a boy who went to Mandy's school. He said he'd overheard Mandy telling his sister that she was running away, that she was going to camp out in the woods until she decided what to do next. We knew the woods he mentioned, so we went there.

'We just wanted to talk to her. We never meant for . . .'

'For what?' asked Jenny, her voice shaking. 'You never meant for what?'

'We called her. "Mandy! Mandy!" We called for ages. There was no answer. We were getting frantic. Then we saw her. She was up a tree. We saw her face, looking down at us.

'"Mandy!" we called. "Come down, we want to talk to you."

'"NO!" she said. "I know what you've been doing. You're going to kill me, aren't you?"

'The funny thing was, it had never occurred to us to kill her. Of course it hadn't. We're not murderers, we're just ordinary people. And yet when she said it, I thought that's what it comes down to, isn't it? Her life or Stephen's. We had enough tissue samples to last us for years. We didn't need her any more. We could make it look like an accident. Nobody would blame us: we were the good guys. We'd taken in this troubled girl from a terrible background, we'd done our best, but she

224

was difficult; it wasn't our fault she ran away. She was a bad one. And with her dead, we could carry on treating Stephen. No one would know.

'Oh Jenny, it was tempting. I won't lie to you. There is nothing stronger than a mother's love. How far would I go to save my only child? But I couldn't do it. I couldn't kill her in cold blood. I thought maybe I could, but in the end I couldn't.

'So I told her, I told her I was sorry, but I just didn't want Stephen to die. I begged her not to tell – that if she told, he would die, and that it would be on her conscience. We gave her money, told her to keep running, to get a flat, get a job, tell people she was older. She looked older than fourteen, and she couldn't wait to leave school anyway.

'So she went. We went home and waited until the next day, and then we told the police that she'd run away. They looked for her but they didn't find her. That was thirty-one years ago.'

Thirty-one years ago.

It was John who spoke next.

'Stephen was perfectly normal and healthy in all ways except one. He stopped ageing. His growth and development remained suspended. We didn't notice at first; sometimes growth slows for no reason and then picks up again. Except his growth hadn't just slowed, it had stopped. We looked at photos from just before the treatment. He hadn't changed a bit. Something in the treatment was causing his body to remain five years old. We were confounded. We didn't know what was causing it, or if it was temporary or what. When two years went by and Stephen still hadn't aged, we were really worried. We had to stop taking him to the GP because he was getting suspicious. Dr Jo agreed to continue to be his primary care-giver. He couldn't go to school – they would notice that he wasn't ageing – so we kept him at home. There were problems at first. Stephen's friend Johnny kept coming around to visit; his mother asked if Stephen would be starting primary school. What could we tell her? I decided that we would home-school Stephen. That would stop him from getting too bored at home and would get Johnny's mother off our backs as well. But she kept bringing Johnny round to visit. It was almost disastrous. We had to pretend we were out, and not return her phone calls. We thought about moving then, but that would have been very difficult. The cell cultures were delicate and transporting them and the lab without attracting attention would have been nearly impossible. Thankfully, Johnny's mother stopped trying to get in touch and we were able to relax a little.

'But John and I were still ageing. And it occurred to us that we would get too old one day to care for Stephen. That's when we decided to try the treatment on ourselves, to see if it would stop us from ageing.

'So we tried it. It was even harder to tell if it was working in us because ageing is less easy to quantify in your thirties. But time would tell. Years passed. We occasionally enrolled Stephen into a nursery school or day care for a year to give us a break from the home-schooling. We would give them false addresses; they weren't very stringent about checking up on their pupils, so we got away with it. Ten years later nothing had changed. We looked great, we felt great. We should have been hitting middle-aged spread, and wrinkles and aches and pains, but we were in the prime of health.

'We had discovered what alchemists and scientists through the ages had searched for and failed to find.

'The elixir of life.

'The fountain of youth.

'Immortality.

'By continually replacing old, tired cells with new young ones, we had defeated ageing. We could still die in an accident, or succumb to illness, but as our research with stem cells is way ahead of conventional science, theoretically we can cure countless more illnesses than current medicine. Without the restraints of ethics committees and government officials, we have leapt forward.

'But we can't tell anyone, because they would make us stop and Stephen would die.'

Jenny was stunned. Fascinated, horrified, elated? She wasn't even sure what she felt. They hadn't killed Mandy at least, so they probably wouldn't kill her. But would they expect her to run away now? She couldn't run away. She had school and physio . . . and Lee.

John went on speaking, his voice assaulting the silence even though he spoke softly.

'We used Mandy's cells for over thirty years. We had to work out ways to avoid being found out. I had to change jobs every so often. We paid for forged birth certificates and other documents. It was harder at first. What did we know about getting illegal documents? It's easy now: we can get anything we want through the internet, now we know where to look.

'We paid off the mortgage on the house, an advantage of long life – we're still young enough to enjoy the fruits of our labours. Helen's pots have made us a lot of money too. I could give up work if I wanted, but I want to keep working in labs so I can see if the rest of the world is anywhere near catching us up yet. Besides, I like work.' A ghost of a smile flickered across John's face, the first sign of levity since the conversation began.

His smile disappeared as quickly as it had come.

'The cells were running out, though. You can only keep growing each batch for so long before errors start occurring in the cell division. They have a "shelf life", if you like. Even the frozen cell lines were running out. So we needed a new donor. The fostering association didn't check records back as far as the 1970s. Why would they need to? As far as they were concerned, we would have been children then. We had forged birth certificates for ourselves and our children, even death certificates for the girls with the dates changed. We showed them photographs of our family. The clothes were old fashioned, but nobody questioned that. We dressed in outdated clothes at our interview so they would think that was just our style. Dr Jo gave us a character reference. Everything went smoothly.

'Lee was the first. Nice boy, very polite – not compatible, though.

'We had a theory that certain physical features seemed to be linked with the cell lines that we wanted: dark hair, dark eyes, slender build. We didn't know if Lee's being Asian would have any effect. The different ethnic groups are closer than you'd think genetically. But it wasn't to be. We told the authorities that we didn't feel Lee had settled in very well with us, but that we'd like to try again, maybe with a girl. They were very understanding. There were two more, girls from a different care home. Neither was a match. Again we said that they just weren't right for our family. Then there was you.

'Jennifer Ackerman. Compatible. Our new saviour.'

Jenny didn't know what to think. Her anger had leached away, to be replaced by . . . what? Pity? Understanding? Still fear. Yes, she was still afraid. Afraid of what she'd heard, afraid of what would happen next. Part of her wanted to get away, far away from the Hollands and their stem-cell therapy. They weren't really her family. She didn't owe them anything; quite the opposite, in fact. And yet she felt tied, obliged to them. Obliged to Stephen, who could die without her.

'Mummy.'

Stephen was in the room. Sleepy and tousle-haired. The visual aid to accompany Jenny's thoughts.

'Did you wake up, love? Are you feeling okay?' Helen held out her arms and Stephen leaned into her, accepting her embrace.

'Can I have some juice please, Mummy?'

'Yes, love, I'll get you some.'

Jenny watched them leave the room, and was suddenly overcome by tiredness. She hadn't slept for more than twenty-four hours, but the adrenalin that had surged through her since leaving the hospital car park had kept her going until now. She tried desperately to stay awake. It was ironic that insomnia had kept her awake when she was safe, but now that she wanted to be alert, she couldn't resist the urge to sleep.

John was looking at her with an expression of concern, but his image was swimming before her eyes. She felt her eyelids getting heavy, and thought briefly that she mustn't go to sleep on the sofa. Mustn't . . . But it was too late. Sleep can only be held back for so long until it claims you, and Jenny was powerless to stop it.

Sixteen

When she woke she was in her bed. It was dark, and she looked over at her alarm clock. Three a.m. The house was quiet. Jenny wondered if John and Helen were sleeping, or if they were working beneath her, manipulating her cells as they had manipulated her.

They must have lifted her into her bed after she'd fallen asleep. Were they gentle? Did they have any feelings towards her other than satisfaction because her cells were a match? Did they look tenderly at her sleeping face as they carried her? Having no legs made her lighter, not too heavy to carry. At least they might have been grateful for that.

She was thirsty, and she needed to go to the toilet. She got into her chair and wheeled out into the hall. Her chair creaked and rattled. So much for tiptoeing. Neither her wheelchair nor her prosthetic legs were made with stealth in mind.

She stopped every few yards and listened.

Silence.

Perhaps everyone *was* sleeping.

Into the bathroom – the toilet flush sounded like a

tidal wave, but still no one stirred.

On to the kitchen, manoeuvring herself to the dishwasher to get a glass, and then to the fridge to get juice. She was hungry now too, and took some leftover cake from the fridge. '– En –' was written on it in Stephen's shaky hand: the remnants of 'Jenny'.

The kitchen light was off, but moonlight came in from the garden. She sat at the table and ate slowly, picking around the letters until they were left like plinths on her plate, with rocky gorges of cake excavated between them. She sipped juice after each mouthful, and thought about what was going on.

Imagine being five years old for more than thirty years, she thought. No wonder Stephen was clever, no wonder he could play the ocarina so well. But why wasn't he more clever, more mature? Because maturity is not just about experience, it's about brain development, she answered for herself. A five-year-old's brain is still a five-year-old's brain, no matter how much experience they have. She remembered a programme she'd once watched about brain development, how little children were really good at learning languages because of the way their brains are wired up. John and Helen should travel the world so that Stephen could learn lots of languages, she thought. But then what's the point of a multilingual five-year-old? It's not as if he could get a job at the United Nations or anything.

How strange, though. Childhood is normally such a transitory time. 'They grow up so quickly' was a phrase she'd heard countless parents mutter, proudly or sadly.

But not Stephen. Stephen would never grow up. Should she pity him, or envy him? Isn't that what Peter Pan wanted? Never to grow up? She remembered how she'd thought of Peter Pan when she'd tried to write a poem about Stephen. Had it been a premonition, or was there an ageless quality about him that she had picked up on? Her subconscious seeing things that her conscious mind did not.

And John and Helen should be in their sixties or even seventies by now. They had really found the key to eternal life.

If the world found out, what would it do? Burn them as heretics, or revere them as saints? Who would get the treatment? Who would be given the gift of eternal life? Everyone? Or just a select few? Those with enough money to afford it perhaps. Or those considered worthy of the honour.

Not murderers or rapists. Not paedophiles. But where would you draw the line? Should someone who'd committed tax fraud have a longer life than someone with speeding tickets? What about overpopulation? Would people stop having children? Or have eternal babies forever sucking at their breasts?

Jenny shuddered at the thought. An eternal baby seemed so wrong, worse even than an eternal five-year-old.

She wouldn't get the treatment. They wouldn't waste it on a cripple. Maybe someone who'd lost one leg, but not two. Would she even want it? The thought put an idea into her head. She could make a deal with John and Helen. I won't tell if you keep me forever young. Would it work using her own stem cells on herself, or would they have to foster another child, drug them and take their cells? Her new 'brother or sister' would never have to know; she would never have found out herself if it weren't for Mandy's diaries.

But what about Lee? He would have to be treated too. She didn't want to stay young without him. But then there was Lee's new family – he was getting along so well, she wouldn't be surprised if they decided to adopt him. So would they need stem cells too? Did they have an extended family, people they wouldn't want to outlive? How far would the ripples travel?

Jenny wondered if John and Helen had had family or friends who had grown old and died without them. They must have offered the treatment to Dr Jo – surely that was the thing she overheard him refusing. Had they offered it to others, or was the threat of being found out too strong a deterrent for them?

Jenny's head was hurting. The pounding pain of disturbed sleep combined with stress to make her wince and massage her temples. No hope of a painkiller. The paracetamol was kept in a high cupboard, making it out of bounds for her in her chair. She could go and get her legs, but she couldn't be bothered.

She finished her cake, finally eating the letters, using the tacky icing to mop up the crumbs on her plate.

Should she go back to bed? She felt that sleep was still far from her, but she wanted to escape at least for a while from the confusing thoughts in her head. Instead, she went to her room and fetched the book she'd been pretending to read for the last few weeks: *Anne of Green Gables*. She took it through to the living room and pulled herself out of her chair and on to the comfortable sofa. She switched on a lamp and settled down to read about the orphan girl whose foster parents were so different from John and Helen. The book was written a hundred years ago in a much simpler time, when nobody knew about cell division or gene therapy. Jenny found it difficult to concentrate on the story, though; always her mind came back to the present, to John and Helen and what was happening to her. She found herself reading the same lines over and over without taking them in. She gave up and put the book down. What will life be like in the year 3000, she wondered. Would she still be alive to see it? Would Stephen still be five years old? She thought of the Robbie Williams song 'I hope I'm old before I die'. Would people stop aging? Would that song seem like nonsense in the new world?

She tried again to read her book, and this time did manage to get into the story, so much so that she didn't notice Helen enter the room and jumped when she said:

'Jenny! Thank goodness! We thought . . .'

'AH!' Jenny shrieked, dropping the book. 'I, um, woke up.'

'When we looked in your room and you weren't there we thought . . . Well, we thought you'd run away. Jenny, promise you won't.'

'Hah,' Jenny laughed, not completely bitterly, but not happily either. 'I'm not really equipped for a life on the street. Or maybe I am – I could get one of those little wheeled beggar platforms, get pity money from passers-by. What d'you think?'

'Jenny! Are you joking? You're not serious?'

'Helen,' Jenny sighed, 'I don't want to run away. I was just getting my life together. I want to pass my GCSEs and my A levels, I want to go to university. I want to be with Lee. And I, well, I was happy here, with you and John and Stephen. I was always a bit suspicious, because of, well, you know, but I thought maybe you liked me, I thought I liked you too. I thought we could be a family.'

'Oh Jenny, we *can* be a family. We have enough cells to last us a long time now, but you could still stay. We do like you, and Stephen loves you. Things needn't change.'

'I don't know, Helen. It's, it's complicated. I don't know what to do.'

Helen smiled, a nervous twitchy smile, and said, 'Okay, you don't need to decide right away. Think about it, talk it over with Lee.'

'You don't mind me telling Lee?'

'Well, John and I thought that if we tell you not to, it'll burn you up inside and you probably will anyway. You must tell him not to tell anyone else, though. Can you trust him?'

'I . . . yeah, I can trust him.'

'Okay, good. You should go back to bed now, try and sleep. I could give you a sleeping tablet.'

Jenny winced at the mention of sleeping tablets.

'I know,' said Helen. 'That's probably the last thing

you want from me. But it might be for the best; you should at least wean yourself off them slowly. I could ask Dr Jo to look at you, decide on the best method. We can trust him.'

'Okay,' said Jenny, 'and maybe a couple of paraceta-mol as well – I've got a killer headache.'

'Sure, I'll bring them for you now.'

It was only after Jenny had taken the tablets and was back in her bedroom, that she wondered what John and Helen had been doing looking for her in her room at four a.m. anyway.

The next day was Sunday and Lee was taking her out. She couldn't wait to see him, not only because she had so much to tell him, but also because his absence had plagued her. He was like an amputated limb and without him she was unbalanced.

He looked exactly the same (well, duh, she thought, it's only been a week).

His foster dad brought him to the house, and waited outside to take them on to town. Helen hugged Lee and Jenny noticed her arms were shaking slightly. John looked nervous too, knowing that Jenny would soon be telling Lee everything that they'd done. She wondered if Lee was picking up on the atmosphere.

Outside in the car Lee said, 'What happened in there? Did you just have a big fight or something?'

'Well, no, not exactly.' Her eyes flicked to the back of Lee's foster dad's head. Lee followed her gaze and then looked back at her, raising his eyebrows questioningly. 'I'll tell you all about it later, okay?'

'Cool.'

She didn't have to wait too long. As soon as Lee's foster dad dropped them in the town, she suggested they go for a coffee. When they were sitting in a cosy nook in the coffee shop, she said, 'Lee, I found out what's going on.'

'What? You mean the big mystery at the Hollands' house? Not more secret phone calls?'

'No! Lee, it's serious, it's . . .' She found herself beginning to lose her composure and impatiently fought back tears. The waitress came along with their two large lattes, which gave her a moment to gather herself.

'You're not going to believe it.'

She told him what she'd read in Mandy's diary on the coach coming home from Austria, and that she'd left it on the bus so that the driver had brought it out and called out Mandy's name. She told him everything John and Helen had admitted to her and he stared at her open-mouthed, his coffee forgotten.

'They were taking cells from you?' Lee looked angry, and Jenny felt warmed by his obvious need to protect her. 'Did it hurt?'

'Well, little things. You should know – they took cells from you too, although they couldn't use yours. The pin prick in my arm. The sore throat from the endoscopy. The bruise on my hip must have been from a bone-marrow biopsy. It's not like it was doing me any harm.' Jenny felt a strange need to defend the Hollands from Lee's anger, although it didn't seem to be working.

'I have to get you out of there. I can't let them do this to you.'

'Lee . . .' Jenny sighed and looked away. 'How can you? If we tell the police, what'll happen to them? What'll happen to Stephen? We can't do that.'

He looked as if he was floundering, helpless to do anything.

'But . . . but . . . but Jenny, you're important too. You don't owe them anything. Why should you let them do this to you?'

'Because I killed my mum! I don't want to kill Stephen too.' Her voice was louder than she intended and several people looked around.

'Very good,' said Lee, loudly enough to be heard by the onlookers, 'now we'll do the scene where the police arrest you, okay?'

The onlookers turned away, satisfied that they'd overheard some sort of play rehearsal.

Then quietly he spoke again.

'Jenny, you know you can't blame yourself. You were just an excited little kid, going skiing. Just like I can't blame myself for not doing anything to stop my parents from getting shot. I was just a little kid, you told me that yourself. It was an accident. A terrible, horrible accident, but it wasn't your fault. Remember what my gran said? It doesn't make you owe anyone anything.'

'I know,' said Jenny. 'I do know now that I can't blame myself, but I still don't want Stephen to die. Not if I can help it.'

They lapsed into silence, deep in thought. The waitress

239

approached the table, but seeing that their cups were still full, moved away again.

Finally Jenny broke the silence. She rummaged in her bag and pulled out a package. 'I got you a present,' she said.

Lee unwrapped the T-shirt she'd bought him and held it up to look at. It was black, with the words 'Jenny in Austria' printed beneath a head and shoulders photo of Jenny looking flushed and mischievous.

'Oh no!' she shrieked, 'I didn't remember the picture being that embarrassing. You have to promise never to wear it.'

'No way,' said Lee. 'I'm gonna wear this every day for the rest of my life.'

'I hope you want a short life then,' Jenny teased, trying to snatch the T-shirt off him. He pushed it underneath himself so he was sitting on it, and then started unbuttoning his shirt.

'Lee! What are you doing? Tell me you're not stripping off in public! Lee!'

He ignored her as he struggled with the complicated manoeuvre of removing his shirt whilst keeping his jacket on over it. He opened the lunch menu that lay on the table and stood it up in front of himself.

'Don't look,' he said. 'I'm shy.'

Jenny was blushing, but giggling too. This was one of the things she loved about Lee: how he could make her laugh even in the most serious of moments.

'The waitress is coming,' she hissed and Lee instantly froze, still hiding behind the menu.

The waitress was middle-aged and tired-looking. She ignored Lee and spoke to Jenny.

'Can I get you anything else?'

'Um, erm . . .'

'Chips!' Lee's voice shot out from behind the menu. Tears streamed down Jenny's face from the laughter she was holding in.

'I'm sorry, um, sir,' the waitress said to the back of the menu, 'we don't do lunches until after twelve.'

'Really,' said Lee, sweeping up the menu to reveal Jenny's face festooned across his chest. 'That's too bad.'

'Just the bill, please,' said Jenny, politely.

The waitress scribbled on a page from her pad and walked away, shaking her head and tutting.

'Lee, you're an idiot!' Jenny whispered, but she was smiling. The first genuine smile since she'd got back from Austria.

'Well, you're an idiot for going out with me then,' he shot back, and leaned across the table to kiss her. 'Thank you,' he said, 'for the T-shirt. I love it.'

They looked at shops and then ate at McDonald's. After lunch they went ten-pin bowling. Jenny had to use the wire ramp to launch her balls, but she insisted that it required just as much skill as throwing them. They were both pretty bad anyway – not that they minded.

John had agreed to pick them up when they were ready, so Jenny used Lee's mobile to ring the Hollands from a bench outside the bowling alley. Their mood had sobered up at the thought of Jenny going back to her foster home. They were both avoiding talking about it, but it hung in the air anyway. When Jenny tried to give Lee his phone back he refused to take it.

'What?' she said. 'I called him, he's coming.'

'I know,' said Lee, 'but I want you to keep the phone. If I can't stop you from going back to the Hollands, at least I can give you this. Hide it, don't let them know you have it, but keep it with you all the time. If they try to do anything to you, ring me. Okay?'

Jenny nodded, and then quickly hid the phone as they saw John's car approaching.

John asked them about their day as he drove to Lee's house. They told him about bowling, and Jenny showed him a CD she'd bought.

'We'll have to get you a CD player for your room,' he said, 'or one of those modern computerised music things.'

'It's all right,' Jenny said. 'I have a personal CD player already that I brought with me.'

'Oh, okay.'

When Lee had been dropped off, Jenny moved into the front of the car, beside John. She wanted to ask him about something that had occurred to her earlier that day.

'John,' she said, as they pulled out of Lee's driveway, 'I've been thinking. About, you know, the stem-cell treatment and stuff.'

'Yes . . .' John sounded hesitant, wondering what was coming next.

'Well, wouldn't it be possible to work out what it is that stops ageing, and what it is that treats Stephen's illness, and like separate them? I mean, would it not be possible to make him well without him staying the same age?'

'Um, well, it . . . that is, it would . . . I mean, yes, but . . . AH!'

John slammed on the brakes and overshot a junction he had not noticed approaching. A passing driver blared his horn and shouted something rude out of his window.

'John?' Jenny pressed the point when John was driving along again. 'Is it possible?'

'I, well . . . it, yes. Theoretically, yes, it is.'

'Then why don't you?'

'Helen doesn't . . . that is, we don't . . . Jenny . . .' John indicated left and pulled the car into a lay-by not far from the Hollands' house. 'Jenny, she doesn't want to lose him. If we stop the treatment, we might age quickly, or the aging might just resume from where it left off. Either way, he will grow up and leave us. And Helen doesn't want that.'

'But John!' Jenny was horrified as she realised what John was saying. 'Stephen has a right to grow up. He wants to. He wants to have a life of his own, to be someone, to do things that only adults can do. You can't take that away from him! It's, it's not right!'

John looked at her but then quickly looked away. He pulled the car back on to the road and said shortly, 'You don't understand.' His eyes were glued to the road, to the traffic, his expression closed.

Jenny did not speak again until they pulled into the driveway.

'Thanks for the lift,' she said.

'You're welcome,' said John, before coming around to her door and handing her her crutches. 'It's the least I can do.'

Seventeen

Jenny spent a long time wondering what she should do. Could she stay with the Hollands, knowing that they were denying Stephen the chance to grow up and have a life of his own? Could she carry on the charade, tricking the little boy who wanted to be bigger? Or should she go to the police, spill the beans on what would be the biggest scientific news of the century – of history – and risk denying Stephen any life at all?

She took the sleeping tablet that Helen gave her at bedtime, but she didn't swallow it; instead, she dropped it into the waste paper bin under the desk in her room. She wanted to stay awake, to experience again that special night-time quiet, the time when her mind seemed most active and she could wrestle with the moral arguments that seemed to escape her in the daytime.

She lay in bed, pretending to sleep until finally John and Helen went upstairs, until the soft noises of their whispering voices, the soft padding of their slippered feet died down and the house was silent.

Then she sat up, supported by warm, soft pillows.

She looked out of her window at the garden. The lawn silver and black in the moonlight, the trees clinging to a few last leaves as autumn turned reluctantly to winter. The stream never resting, finding its well-worn paths over rocks and through gullies. The moon, bright and benevolent, its familiar face looking down as if it were smiling and offering hope of a better future.

And without fretting and reasoning, the solution came to her. She knew what she must do, and the knowledge calmed her.

'I'll do it tomorrow,' she said. And for the first time in months her body drifted peacefully and easily into a deep natural sleep.

She sought out Hayley at school the next day and used a payphone to call Sarah at Oak Hall.

She spent an anxious couple of hours waiting for home time before she could ring Sarah back and see if she'd been able to speak to Hayley's foster parents. Sarah was non-committal, uncertain about making any arrangements before she'd spoken to the Hollands, but Jenny said she just wanted to be sure that it was possible before her foster parents were told. She finally persuaded Sarah to wait before phoning them and to sort out the other things first.

She had a couple of other things she wanted to do before the Hollands learned about her plans.

When she got home, she took a drink into her room and told Helen she had 'masses of homework'.

In fact, her homework was light and she did it quickly, getting it out of the way before settling down to the real task.

She took from a drawer in her desk a paper bag containing a notebook. It was identical to the ones she wrote her poetry in, except that it had not yet been started. On the cover she wrote:

TO THE NEXT FOSTER CHILD OF THE HOLLANDS.

On the inside cover she wrote:

> I want to tell you a story. It's a long story that began way back in the 1970s. Sometimes it's sad, or difficult to understand, but it's important, and you need to know it to understand what may be happening to you. Please don't tell the Hollands anything about this book – at least, not until you've read it all and made up your own mind about what you should do.

Satisfied with the introduction, she flattened out the blank first page, chewing the end of her pen while she wondered how the story should begin.

She started with what John had told her, about Lindsay getting hurt, the Hollands taking her to the hospital, the doctor giving them the bad news. She talked about their attempts to find a cure, their frustrations at the limits put on them by the government, about the deaths of their two daughters. She tried to be fair, to relay the facts without spinning them to push the reader's sympathies one way or another. She wanted to give them enough detail so that they would understand, so that they would have time for it to sink in and not instantly fly off the handle, but not so much that they got bored before realising their part in the story.

She paused to rest her hand and her mind, before taking a deep breath and ploughing on.

> So Helen had had the idea to foster. To look for children whose cell types matched Stephen's, and harvest stem cells from them . . . after a few failed attempts, they found a match. Her name was Amanda Patterson.

Jenny again paused. What should she say about Mandy? Was there any need for this hypothetical future foster child to know her story? Did it matter that her dad was in prison, and her mum had had a breakdown?

It mattered to Jenny, but ultimately she thought, no, she didn't need to tell Mandy's story here.

So instead she told how the therapy worked, how Stephen got better, but how it had the unexpected side effect of stopping him from ageing.

She told them how the Hollands had used it on themselves, freezing their little nuclear family in time. She listed the signs that would show the person reading if their cells were being taken: the needle hole in the inner elbow, the sore throat from endoscopy, the hip bruising from biopsy. It occurred to her that techniques might have changed by the time the Hollands fostered again, so she mentioned that, and told the reader to look out for any unexplained scars or injuries that might be sites of cell removal.

And then she told them the thing that had finally made her feel she couldn't stay with the Hollands, the thing that she couldn't justify. That they could treat Stephen without keeping him as a child, but that they chose not to.

She explained her own part in the story, and what she'd decided to do. She said she would try to set up a web page and keep checking in case the person reading this wanted to contact her. Then she closed the book.

She was wearing her legs, so she walked over to her bedroom door and dropped her heavy schoolbag in front of it. It wouldn't stop a determined person from opening the door, but it would at least slow them down enough to give her warning. That done, she lowered herself down to the ground, and slid under the bed. She found the floorboard that moved, and dropped the notebook into the secret niche beneath it, uttering a silent prayer that it would remain there until it was found by someone who needed to read it.

Then she slid back out, and brushed off the dust. She moved her bag away from the door, and sat back down at the desk. There was one more letter she wanted to write, and it would be even harder than the first.

She still wasn't sure if this was the right thing to do, if she had any right to interfere in how John and Helen chose to care for their son. And yet she felt some solidarity with Stephen: he was like a brother to her, and he had confided in her. He had wished to be bigger.

Was he too young to understand? She didn't know. But if he never would be any older, was that a good enough reason to keep the truth from him?

I'll write it, she thought, and then I'll decide whether or not to give it to him.

This time she wrote on an A4 sheet, taken from her school notepad.

She began:

Dear Stephen

I'm going to tell you a secret, so you mustn't tell Mummy and Daddy, at least not until you've thought about it for a long time, and you're sure that you understand it properly. I know that you're a very clever and good boy, so you'll know when you've thought about it enough.

The first bit isn't a secret, but it's still important to remember, and that is that your Mummy and Daddy love you very much indeed, and that everything they do for you and to you is because of how much they love you.

The second bit is about your sisters. Do you remember that your sisters died a very long time ago, and that that made your Mummy and Daddy very sad? Well, an even sadder thing is that you were sick too, and you were going to die too. Your Mummy and Daddy worked very hard to find a medicine that would make you better, and they did find it, and gave it to you and it did make you better.

But the funny thing was that as well as making you better, the medicine made you stop growing up. Did you know that other little boys and girls have a birthday once a year? And each time they have a birthday they are one year older? Did you know that every time Christmas comes along you should be one year older? And did you know that most boys and girls go to school and every year they go to different classes and learn new things, and they get taller and older until one day they leave school and maybe get a job or go to university? And maybe they get married or travel the world, or do other things that only grown-ups can do.

Stephen, when your Mummy and Daddy first made the medicine, they didn't know that it was going to stop you from getting older. When they found out, they thought that it was better for you to be healthy and keep taking the medicine, than for you to get sick and die. And your Mummy and Daddy took the medicine too, so they wouldn't get too old to look after you.

But Stephen (and this is the really important bit that you need to think about very hard), they found a way to make you better without stopping you from growing up.

Now you might wonder why they haven't given you the new medicine, and why you haven't started getting bigger, and to understand that you need to remember how sad your Mummy and Daddy were when your sisters died.

Because your parents love you so much, they feel afraid that if you grow up, you'll leave them . . . and even though that's much better than you dying, it still makes them feel like they're losing you. Do you understand? It's like when you felt sad about your friend Johnny not coming to visit you any more, even though Johnny didn't die. That's how your parents feel.

Do you know what I think, Stephen? I think that if you talked to your parents, and told them how you felt about growing up, that they might change their minds and feel proud and happy about you getting bigger. But you need to be very careful not to upset them or make them angry. Can you do that?

I want you to know, Stephen, that I love you too, maybe almost as much as your Mummy and Daddy do, and I'm sorry that I had to go away. I felt bad about the medicine stopping you from growing up, and that's why I left, not because of you.

I'd love it if you wrote me letters, or came to visit me, although I think your Mummy and Daddy might be cross with me if they find out I told you about the medicine. If they are cross though, don't worry. I know it's not your fault and I will always love you.

I will keep trying to play the ocarina and it will always make me think of you.

With lots of love,
Jenny
xxx

Jenny read over the note and she was crying by the time she got to the end. She folded it and slipped it into Stephen's copy of *The Wishing Chair* that she'd taken from his room earlier. She heard a noise outside and looked up to see Stephen and Helen in the garden, stomping through piles of dried leaves and laughing together.

For a moment she wavered, looking at their happy faces, but the moment passed and she resolved to seize the opportunity and put the book on Stephen's bedside table while there was no danger of her being intercepted.

Her heart was beating fast when she left his room, and the sound of the phone ringing made her jump.

She answered it, and heard Sarah's voice on the other end of the line. She wanted to speak to Helen, but Jenny asked if she could have a few minutes to speak to her first. Sarah said that was okay, and that she would ring back. Jenny was just hanging up when Stephen and Helen came back in through the kitchen door.

'Who was on the phone?' Helen asked.

'It was Sarah, from Oak Hall,' Jenny said. 'Helen, can I talk to you?'

She looked meaningfully at Stephen, and Helen took the hint and sent him off to spend half an hour on the computer.

'Cool!' said Stephen. 'Can I play maths challenge?'

'Yes, love.'

Helen closed the kitchen door after him, and then turned to Jenny.

'I rang Sarah earlier,' she began, 'asked her to talk to Hayley's foster parents. Hayley's been asking since before I even came here if I could go and live with them. Because we were roommates, you know, like sisters. And I've decided that I do want to. I . . .' Her eyes wandered and she couldn't meet Helen's gaze. 'I'm sorry, Helen, I really am. I do love you and John and Stephen, but I don't feel . . . because of everything . . . But I didn't tell anyone. Except Lee, and I won't tell anyone else. I'll tell them that I was very happy here, and I *was* very happy here. But I'll say I missed Hayley too much. That's all. Is that okay?'

'I guess I can understand why you want to leave,' Helen said. 'It must be hard for you to trust us now. We'll be sorry to lose you, though, truly. Do you know what Hayley's family think about this?'

'Sarah spoke to them. They're happy, excited. I'm quite a novelty.'

Helen smiled. 'Jenny, you're not a novelty. You're just a lovely girl, and I'm sorry that we used you, but I'm glad that we got to know you.'

'Yeah, me too,' said Jenny. 'Sorry but glad as well.'

Epilogue

My foster sister, Hayley, gave me this diary for Christmas. I've never really kept a diary, just notebooks full of poems and stuff. But here goes.

I got loads of presents this year. Clothes, books, my own potter's wheel and set of clay tools (coolest present ever). I got a book from my last foster brother, Stephen: The Wishing Chair by Enid Blyton. I'd left a note for him in his copy of it, so I think it was his way of telling me that he'd read it. Lee gave me a silver charm bracelet (Lee is my gorgeous boyfriend as seen in the photo on the front cover. He's the one holding the crutches, although, before you ask, he has all his bits. The crutches are mine.)

Let me introduce myself. My name is Jennifer Moonchild Firstjoy Ackerman (but if you tell anyone about my middle names I'll kill you).

I'm nearly fifteen. I've just moved in with a new foster family called the Johnstons. They fostered my roommate from the children's home where I used to live, and now they foster me too. My last foster home didn't work out. I might tell you about that some time.

My hobbies are:

Kissing Lee, writing poetry, drawing, kissing Lee, pottery, playing the ocarina, kissing Lee, reading, skiing, kissing Lee, being a TV personality . . . well, all right, I'm not exactly a TV personality, but I am in a documentary that's going to be shown on the TV in a few weeks. Having seen it already, I have to say that I'm brilliant in it.

In case you're wondering, the documentary is about my skiing trip, because it was the first British skiing trip for kids with arm or leg amputations. I am a double above the knee amputee, and a wicked skier. That sounds like the start of a joke, doesn't it: 'Did you hear the one about the no-legged skier . . . ?' But seriously, it's true. Paralympics here I come . . .

I've just decided what I want to do with my life – well, apart from being absolutely brilliant at all my hobbies (I think I need more practice at kissing Lee though!).

I want to be a doctor.

I'm clever enough (even though I say so myself) and hard-working, and that's what I want to do, so I'm going for it. I think Eve, that's my mum who died, would be proud of me. I think that would make her happy. Lee can support me through medical school, and then he can give up work and look after our children while I push forward the boundaries of medicine.

I'm so excited.

Roll on rest of my life.

I can't wait!

Acknowledgements

I'd like to thank Don Cummings from the prosthetics department at Texas Scottish Rite Hospital for Children, for his technical input, and especially for sharing his experiences of skiing with amputee children.

I'd also like to thank everyone involved in the Wow Factor Competition, especially my wonderful editor Julia Wells. It was such a brilliant opportunity for an unknown writer like myself to get noticed. It has certainly changed my life. Thank you.